Stirrings of the Dead

"Listen!" A thin finger went to Miss Collingwood's lips. "She's here. Mrs. Kirkwood. Upstairs. Walking."

"My aunt is dead," said Jennifer, the words not coming out as she had wanted them to. Her voice trembled.

"She's come back," said Miss Collingwood, her hand at her throat. "She's come back from the dead. And she's walking upstairs."

**OTHER MANOR BOOKS
BY
FLORENCE HURD**

**Curse Of The Moors
Moorsend Manor**

Terror At Seacliff Pines

Florence Hurd

MANOR
BOOKS
INC.

A MANOR BOOK......1976

Manor Books Inc.
432 Park Avenue South
New York, New York 10016

CHAPTER I

Jennifer flinched inwardly as the iron gates of the elevator clanged shut behind her. Gazing around at the cracked tile and peeling plaster of the walls, she had the feeling that Hester's lawyer's choice of an office building probably reflected the economic status of his clients. Her deceased great-aunt's estate was undoubtedly worth little, if anything. Yet, Jennifer thought that there was always the slim chance she had guessed wrong.

She turned left and began to walk down a corridor, lined on either side with frosted glass doors, her footsteps clap-clapping on the cold, marbled floor. The dimly lit hallway had the odor of disinfectant and echoed silence, a silence devoid of the customary sounds Jennifer associated with business offices: clacking typewriters, humming voices, the shrill ring of telephones. The dead quiet gave her an odd feeling, a strange sense of having walked here before, in a dream perhaps. "I shouldn't have come," she thought suddenly, feeling inexplicably anxious and lost.

But the sensation was fleeting, and in the next moment she was standing in front of the opaque glass door bearing the legend: JAMES P. EMMETT, ATTORNEY AT LAW.

The small, shabby waiting room contained a

tired, black leather sofa, flanked by two scarred end tables each holding an ecru-shaded lamp and a few tattered copies of *National Geographic*. From behind a partition a middle aged receptionist at a typewriter looked up questioningly.

"I have an appointment with Mr. Emmett," Jennifer said, thinking Aunt Hester had probably left boxes of junk jewelry, old theatre programs and faded photographs, pictures of people Jennifer had never known and never seen, miscellany she would not know what to do with. "I'm Jennifer Sargent."

"Oh yes," said the woman, glancing across at an open appointment book. "He's expecting you. Second door to your left."

The second door to the left was closed, and Jennifer tapped on it.

"Come in."

Mr. Emmett was very much like Jennifer's mental picture of him, elderly, lean, with bony, ink-stained fingers and a scholarly air.

"Yes?" he said in some surprise.

"I'm Miss Sargent," Jennifer said. "I spoke to you over the phone about the ad in the paper?" His eyebrows, like two, white hairy wings remained poised over his watery, spectacled eyes. "The ad asking for the relatives of Hester Kirkwood to get in touch with you. I'm the great-niece."

"Oh yes, yes. Dear me, yes. Do be seated, Miss...?"

"Sargent." She sat down and immediately snagged one of her stockings on the chair's splintery leg.

Across from her Mr. Emmett opened a desk drawer and took out a manila folder. "Kirkwood,"

6

he muttered, "yes, yes," then lifting his gaze, "You have brought identification?"

"I have it here." She put the large white envelope that she had been carrying clutched tightly under her arm, on the desk and from it extracted her birth certificate, copies of her grammar and high school registration, her parent's marriage license, and her mother's birth certificate.

Mr. Emmett spread the documents out and began to study each carefully, lifting them one by one with thin, fastidious fingers.

Jennifer's eyes slid to the clock on the wall. She had thirty minutes left of her lunch hour.

When she had first read the ad, she had reacted with instant excitement; but ever since she had spoken to Mr. Emmett over the phone, her excitement had begun to dribble away until now she only felt tense and impatient. If she were late, Mr. Goodbody would pout.

"Your mother was the deceased's niece, then?" Mr. Emmett inquired.

"Yes. Hester Kirkwood was my great-aunt." And then feeling that she ought to show more than a pecuniary interest in a relative's death; even though their acquaintanceship had been slight, she asked: "When did Mrs. Kirkwood die?"

"Three weeks ago. The twelfth of May, I believe it was. Hmmmm. Have you a driver's license?"

"Yes." She got it out of her wallet and gave it to him.

Actually she had only seen Hester once, long ago. How long, Jennifer did not know. She was ten at the time, so it must have been close to fourteen years since the day she, her mother and Aunt

Hester had lunch in Kostloff's, a greasy spoon tucked in between a tie shop and drug store on Randolph Street. Aunt Hester, then living in California, had been on the stage in her youth and had returned to visit old haunts in Chicago, her native city. Jennifer had been very impressed with Hester, noting with precocious eyes that her great aunt seemed younger than her mother. Perhaps it was because her mother's face always wore a frown, the air of martyrdom befitting a woman deserted by her husband after two years of marriage; left alone to rear the infant Jennifer; forced to make her way in a world from which, until then, she had managed to be protected. Or perhaps it was because of Hester's outlandish, rather garish appearance, the highly rouged cheeks, the bright, lipsticked mouth, the green lidded eyes, the dozens of gold bracelets on her arm, clanking and jingling as she kept moving them up and down in a habitual, nervous gesture. The black dress she wore (mourning for her husband, Hubert, who had died years earlier) and trailing yards of floating chiffon at the throat and the wrists seemed to heighten the woman's glamour in Jennifer's childish mind. Hester spoke of her deceased husband with an endearing romanticism which Jennifer's mother had never used for her own spouse. "Hubert did not leave me much," Jennifer recalled Hester's deep, soulful sigh as she spoke, "except lovely memories."

Memories, Jennifer thought she should have remembered that before she had gone dashing madly about, gathering the paraphernalia of identification together, all the while daydreaming of fantastic riches falling in her lap. Hester's death

8

was sad, but remote, and Jennifer should not have expected more from it than a passing nostalgic thought or two.

"I believe these pretty well authenticate your claim," Mr. Emmett said, pursing his thin lips.

"Were there others who answered the ad?" Jennifer wanted to know.

"Yes, quite a few. There always are. All imposters." He dismissed the imposters with a wave of his bony hand.

"What I can't understand," Jennifer said, "is why there was an ad in the first place? My mother is dead, that's true. But my name is still the same, and I'm in the phone book. I don't believe my great-aunt had any other relatives." They had never heard from Aunt Hester again since that afternoon; although Jennifer's mother had written several times.

"I don't really know why," Mr. Emmett said, stroking his chin, looking down at the opened manila folder. "Actually I was barely acquainted with Mrs. Kirkwood. It was her husband, Hubert, who had once been my client." He made a few notations on a yellow pad, his pen skimming over the paper, making spidery hieroglyphics.

Jennifer's eyes went to the clock again. Lordy, it was ten to one! She would not only be late, but good and late. Goodbody would either dock her pay or insist she make it up in overtime.

"There isn't any money, I'm afraid," Mr. Emmett said. Jennifer expected that as she vaguely recalled, that uncle Hubert had been in patent medicines, corn plasters, or something like that. "But there is a house, Seacliff Pines, and five acres of grounds."

"A house and grounds?" Jennifer suddenly sat up.

"I have never seen it. But the property as described here is on a bluff right over the water. It is located...let me see...oh, yes, seventy miles south of San Francisco on the Coast Highway."

"What kind of house?" Jennifer asked, leaning forward.

"Kind of house? I'm afraid there's no description, no photograph. And I have no idea of its worth. However, I am given to understand that property in California, especially ocean-view property, commands a high price."

"Can I sell it?" Jennifer asked, the dingy walls of Mr. Emmett's office retreating before the wide, beautiful landscapes suddenly opened to her. "There's no clause saying I have to live in it?" Her eccentric, bracelet-jangling great-aunt could well have put such a stipulation in the will.

"No," said Mr. Emmett. "There seems to be no reason why you can't dispose of it as you wish."

"Good," said Jennifer happily. Her fantasies might be realized yet. She'd quit her job. That was number one on her list. In her mind she could see herself marching boldly into Mr. Goodbody's plastic-paneled office where he sat enthroned behind a plastic desk. She'd tell him he could start looking for another slave, that *she* wouldn't be around anymore, and... "Have you any idea," she asked, "what property sells for out there?" Out there. To Jennifer, born and raised in Chicago and with no discernible hope of ever leaving it, California seemed like an exotic place, palm trees and orange groves and sunshine three hundred sixty-five days of the year.

10

"It just so happens that only last week a client of mine who dabbles in California real estate informed me that he paid twenty thousand dollars for a lot."

Twenty thousand! Jennifer's mind began to leap and cavort in wild mathematical equations. Five acres times twenty thousand...No, not acres—lots. How many lots in an acre? She not only could give up her job, she would be rich. She could spend the next five years traveling, or she could buy a boutique, a smart elegant dress shop. Or if she invested her money right...

"Of course, you understand," Mr. Emmett was saying, "there are restrictions on subdividing, zoning laws, etcetera. However, I'm sure you could realize a substantial sum. If you wish, I'll consult my client for a reliable realtor in that area who could handle the entire transaction for you."

"I'd have to pay him?"

"Why, yes." He said with a thin, quivering smile. "There's a percentage of the sale price, ten per cent for the house, five for bare land."

She thought a moment. "No. No, I think I'd prefer dealing with the matter myself." All she needed was the money for a plane ticket and a few dollars extra to tide her over until she got rid of the house. If what Mr. Emmett said was true, the property would sell quickly, and the realtor's commission would be hers too.

"There will be a few legal formalities," Mr. Emmett said. "But I think we can manage to clear the estate in short order."

"Short order? How long would short order take?" Now that she had rearranged her life, she was impatient to be off. There was nothing and no one to hold her. Her job as executive secretary, an euphemism for maid-of-all-work, to Mr. Goodbody of Goodbody's Appliances, was one she would leave with joy. She had no living relatives. Her love life was stalled at zero. It had been a month since she had broken up with her boyfriend, Jay, a divorced dentist in his thirties, whose idea of a fun evening was to sit in front of the television set with a beer and watch basketball. And no one new had appeared on the horizon. Her only real friend, Louise, had married and moved away to Dubuque. No, there was no one to whom she would regret saying good-bye.

"Seven to nine months," Mr. Emmett said.

"Oh." Jennifer tried not to show her disappointment.

"According to the terms of the will, the advertisement must run for a full month, and then there is probate. If there are no other claimants, I think I may be able to hurry things along."

"I'd appreciate that."

"Very well, then I'll have my secretary call when the deeds are ready for signing."

"Yes..." He held out his hand, and she shook it. "Thank you. Shall I leave these?" She indicated the documents she had brought.

"If you will. I'll have copies made and return them to you."

She was at the door when she suddenly remembered to ask, "Is the house empty? What I mean, is—are there—tenants, renters?"

"Oh, I am sorry, I forgot to tell you. There isn't a tenant, but Mrs. Kirkwood's housekeeper is still on the premises. Her name is Miss Collingwood. She has received a small bequest and permission to

12

remain in the house until it is sold. I shall write to her, of course, and tell her to expect you in, say, seven or eight months."

"Do you suppose there will be any complications?" Jennifer asked, envisioning a tight lipped, granite chinned, family-retainer type in the person of Miss Collingwood.

"Not at all. Miss Collingwood has been well paid according to the terms of the will, and I'm sure she is more than ready to retire. I can't see that there will be any complications."

But there were complications, the sort of complications that neither Mr. Emmett nor Jennifer could have possibly foreseen.

CHAPTER II

Seven months later Jennifer arrived in San Francisco on a sullen November afternoon. Though the weather was no warmer or sunnier than what she had left in Chicago, the gray, low-slung clouds seemed gilded with promise. The cold wind, whipping around corners and down steep inclined streets in chilling blasts, stung Jennifer's cheeks into pink excitement. She had fallen in love with the city at first sight. Everything she saw thrilled and amazed her; the flower stalls, the magnificent airy span of the Golden Gate, the houses stuck together marching up and down the hills, the little fascinating shops tucked away in odd corners.

She wanted to stay for a week at least, before going on to Seacliff Pines, but the house nagged at her. Though probate had not yet been completed, no other claimants had come forward, and Mr. Emmett was reasonably certain that Jennifer was sole heir to the Kirkwood estate. At any rate, unable to wait until all the final, legal details—whatever they were—had been settled, she quit her job, sold her car, gathered what money she could and came West. She was anxious to see the house. She hadn't the vaguest notion of its size, its age, or even its style of architecture. She had sent a letter to Miss Collingwood, the housekeeper, hoping to

get more information, but had never recei
reply.

All she knew of the house was the address: 11423 Coast Highway, Torrey. Ostensibly, Torrey was a town because it had a post office, and it was on the map. She was somewhat dismayed, however, to learn that there was no public transportation, no bus or train which could take her farther south along the coast than Carmel. Perhaps, there, she reasoned, she might be able to hire a car or a cab.

But when she arrived at Carmel, a flowered jewel of a town set beside a jade green sea, an art festival was in progress and literally nothing on wheels was available for renting. In a little courtyard restaurant at lunch she met a raw boned, spinster school teacher from Portland, Maine, who didn't care much for art festivals and offered to drive Jennifer, an offer which she gratefully accepted. It was not until they were well out of Carmel, speeding along the coast, under a canopy of lofty redwoods that Jennifer realized the school teacher was blind drunk. It took another ten minutes, and a near head-on collision with a car rounding a curve, before Jennifer got up the nerve to ask the woman to stop.

"It's right up that dirt road," Jennifer lied, pointing with her chin. In one hurried movement she reached back for her suitcase and her coat and got out of the car.

To her relief the woman didn't argue, but instead made a quick U-turn with a screeching of tires and drove off. Jennifer, alone by the side of the road, watched as the car disappeared.

It was a Wednesday—and November, and the coast road, so busy during the tourist jammed

15

summer months, had little traffic now. Jennifer felt uncomfortably conspicuous. She thought about walking, but she guessed it was at least twenty miles to Torrey and too far to walk. The idea of hitchhiking did not appeal to her, in fact, it was a little frightening; but she had no other choice.

As she saw a car approaching from the distance, all the lurid tales she'd read of robbery, mugging and rape, filled her mind. In a panic she ducked behind a tree. When the car whizzed by, she came out feeling foolish and ashamed. She forced herself out onto the road's shoulder, determined to try and stop the very next car. If she didn't like what she saw—a man alone was definitely out—she needn't accept a ride.

To her surprise three cars sped by, one following the other, leaving her with an odd feeling of rejection. That combined with irritation made her bolder. When the whine of the next car reached her, she stepped smartly out with her thumb. The car, an old Buick with a dented fender, screeched to a halt a couple of yards ahead of her, then backed up. Through the rear window she saw that the driver was a man, and he was alone. When the car came abreast of her, he rolled down the window. "Could I give you a lift?" He was a pleasant looking young man in his late twenties with auburn hair, friendly brown eyes and a nice smile. He did look harmless, but....

Suddenly a dog raised itself in the back seat, a mammoth, white hairy dog, so hairy, the eyes and face were hidden. Only black button-like nostrils indicated that the animal was front ended.

"What kind of dog is that?" Jennifer asked, laughing.

"That's Rena, an English sheep dog. Haven't you seen one before?" He reached back and patted the dog.

"No."

The dog began to pant, a large, pink tongue lolling beneath thick fronds of white hair. "She's warm," the man said, patting her again. Then turning to Jennifer, "I'm going just a mile beyond Torrey. Will that help?"

She hesitated. A man who likes dogs can't be all bad, she told herself. "That's just fine." Smiling reassuringly, he reached across and opened the door. Picking up her suitcase, Jennifer got in.

She did not regret her decision. She felt comfortable with him from the start. They exchanged names—his was John McGraw, and he was a part-time potter.

"Part-time?" Jennifer asked.

"Yes, ceramics don't pay much. Not in this area where every other man, woman and child throws pots. And some of them are real pros. So in order to buy groceries, I sell real estate on the side."

"Real estate. Well, now isn't that a coincidence!" She laughed. "Would you like to buy a house?"

"Don't tell me you're in real estate too." He had long sideburns which gave his face a rather solemn look when he wasn't smiling.

"No," she said. "I just have the one house to sell. Seacliff Pines. Do you know it?"

"Know it? It's practically next door, if you call a half-mile next door. Let's say I know of it. I once tried to get Mrs. Kirkwood to list it with me, that's when I was new and out ringing doorbells to drum up business, and she drove me off the property with a gun." He shook his head. "I'm not likely to forget that in a hurry. But..." turning to her,

17

"you...you *did* say you were selling it, didn't you?"

"Yes. Seacliff Pines is mine. Mrs. Kirkwood was my great-aunt, and she died and left me the house."

"She died?"

"Yes—about seven months ago. Didn't you know?"

"No," he said, surprised. "I didn't. But then she was a hermit, from what I heard. Didn't have any friends, never went out. I only saw her that once."

"She had—still has—a housekeeper, Miss Collingwood?"

He shook his head. "I had no idea. I might have seen her at the general store in Torrey, but a lot of tourists come through; and though Torrey's just a bend in the road, it's not the kind of place where everybody knows everybody else."

They were silent as the car began to climb. On her right Jennifer caught tantalizing glimpses of the sea, and on her left the yellowed grass-covered cliffs rose, lined with green willows, screening hidden streams.

"How do you like our scenery?" John asked conversationally.

"It's lovely—but where are the palm trees and the oranges?"

He laughed. "There are some, but we're too far north for that kind of tropical stuff."

The car coughed and knocked upward, and when it reached the hairpin turn at the top, they bumped off the road onto a wide, graveled ledge. John shut off the car and reached across to open Jennifer's door. "What do you think of that?"

Jennifer looked down and gasped. "It's...it's beautiful."

18

The wide, wide sea spread before her, shimmering in glassy blue brilliance, melting with the distant horizon. Directly below, far, far below, the translucent, emerald water seemed to break in slow motion, creaming foam over a spired cluster of rocks.

"If you look closely," said John, "there's a sea lion sunning himself on the rocks."

Jennifer stared and then saw it, a dark gray shape, next to the spire. "I've never seen one outside a zoo," Jennifer said. As she spoke the shape moved clumsily, sliding over the rocks and plunged into the sea. "Well, I'll be....!" Jennifer exclaimed. She saw its shadow, swimming gracefully away, in the clear blue water.

John beamed at her as if he himself had arranged the view and its attendant wild life show. He started the car, and they got back on the road, rounding the curve and zig-zagging downward, crossing a long, stone bridge beneath which the water boiled in a rocky chasm.

"I haven't seen a single house yet," Jennifer observed. "Doesn't anyone live along here?"

"There are some homes up in the hills and among the trees," said John, "but you can't see them from the road."

"Seacliff Pines is hidden too?"

"Yes."

"What's the house like?"

"I never really got a good look at it," he said, after a momentary hesitation. "Your great-aunt caught me just inside the gate."

The ribboned road wound down and up and around and down again, always the sun shattered sea on the right, the steep buff-colored hills on the left.

John slowed the car as they approached a long, low, wooden building with several gas pumps out in front. A sign above it read, "Torrey General Store and P.O." Next to it was another building, similarly weather-beaten, announcing "EATS" on a lollipop neon which revolved slowly.

"Behold Torrey," John said. "Need anything?"

"No, thanks. How much further?"

"About three miles."

"You're not going out of your way?"

"Only a half-mile or so. I really don't mind."

Eight minutes later, they pulled up to a crooked wire fence, sagging with morning glories and honey suckle vines. A rust pitted mailbox on a tilted stick, bore the faded name, "Kirkwood".

"If you'll get the gates," John said, "I'll drive you down."

"No, that won't be necessary. No, really. I've taken you out of your way as it is."

John got out and opened the car door for her, then reached for her bag. He was nice, Jennifer thought. She couldn't remember when a man had last exerted himself by opening a door for her.

"I hope," he said, "this is not the end, but the beginning of a friendship. I'll see you again?"

"Yes—I'd like that." She smiled at him, thinking that there was no reason why she couldn't mix business with pleasure.

"Tomorrow night? I'm a terrific cook, and Rena and I would love to have you over for dinner."

Rena, hearing her name, heaved her panting bulk upward, and stuck her shaggy head out the window. "That sounds fine," Jennifer said, rubbing the dog's nose. "But maybe you'd better call first."

He looked past her, his eyes unfocused for a moment. "I don't think that house has a telephone. Telephones are hard to come by in these parts. I don't have one either. Tell you what, why don't I just come over and if you aren't free, well, we'll make it some other time."

"All right."

"And, Jennifer, if you need help in the meantime..."

"What kind of help?"

He shrugged. "I don't know. Leaky faucets. Maybe your great-aunt kept a mean dog. Sure you wouldn't like me to walk you to the door?"

"No—I can manage. And I'm not afraid of dogs."

"Okay, see you tomorrow."

He got into the car, and she waved as he drove off.

The sun had gone behind a cloud, and a cool breeze played with her long hair, fluttering the collar of her blouse. Insects chirped and sang in the tall, bearded weeds by the side of the road, busy frenetic sounds emanating from a world apart making Jennifer feel inexplicably lonely as if she had been suddenly, and through no fault of her own, cast adrift.

She picked up her suitcase and pushed at the gate. It squeaked, buckled, but refused to give. She saw the small padlock then, rusted as was the chain it was fastened to. Somewhat irritated (she had dropped a postcard to Miss Collingwood giving the approximate date of her arrival) she shoved at the gate again, and the rotted padlock suddenly snapped. She unhooked it from the chain, opened the gate and closed it behind her.

A rutted, earth-packed drive went steeply down under interlacing branches of dark pine and oak. She began to feel anxious as she walked. After months of waiting, after numerous—and toward the last, daily—calls to Mr. Emmett, wanting to know if the house was hers, she was going to see it at last. And yet—she wished she had allowed John to drive her to the door.

It was chilly and strangely quiet under the trees. No wind rustled the leaves; no bird twittered; no insects sang as they had in the tall, dried grass beyond the gate. Only the unseen breaking surf could be heard, a far distant rumble, deep and ominous.

Shivering, she set the suitcase down and threw the coat she had been carrying across her arm, around her shoulders. On either side of her the pepper trees and ancient oaks with their gnarled and twisted trunks vied with the gloomy pines in their upward, silent struggle for sun and air. And in between the trees, creeping vines and nameless shrubs joined, intermingled and climbed to make a thick jungle growth, tremulous with moving shadows. She shivered again and picking up her suitcase, quickened her pace, stumbling over a half buried tree root in her haste. Though the air was chill, she was conscious that her hand holding the suitcase had become damp with sweat.

The drive took a jog and continued downward, the trees pressing closer, narrowing the way. She had thought the house might be situated close to the beach, but the sound of the sea remained the same—a muffled, far distant boom. And for a while she had the illusion that she was walking in a circle and would soon emerge at the rusted gate again. But the dirt drive gradually gave way to gray gravel dotted with fringed dandelion weeds, and through the trees she caught a glimpse of a brown wall and a high, narrow window. Then, as the trees suddenly parted, she found herself standing face to face with Seacliff Pines.

The house was a shock. It was incredibly ugly, the ugliest house she had ever seen. A gingerbread monstrosity, it loomed three stories above her, a turreted attic tower making up a fourth. There were two chimneys, flanked by ornate, iron finials and windows of various shapes, round, octagonal, ovoid, curtained like lidded eyes. Sun, wind and rain had streaked the outer walls, fading them, leaving patches of leprous tan beneath the gutters. It was a house that seemed to have been thrown together without forethought, on a malevolent whim, perhaps; though it was far from whimsical. Perhaps a madman had conceived it, the oddly angled walls, the recessed, misshapen windows watching and waiting with suppressed maniacal laughter.

She should have known the house would be so. Wasn't it her mother who was fond of saying, "You can't get something for nothing"? Jennifer's impulse was to turn back, to retrace her steps under the trees, go back beyond the rusted gate and to the sound of the humming, lively insects, back to the road which led to cities peopled in sane and substantial houses.

But *this* is what she had come for, why she had journeyed all these miles to claim her inheritance, for better or for worse.

A dry rustling sound startled her, and looking down, she saw a lizard scuttling across the fallen, brown pine needles. Stirred to action, she took a firmer grip of her suitcase and marched up the four, wide, sagging steps, her footsteps clattering as she crossed the veranda. She put her finger to the door bell, and the ring, a harsh, whirring sound, parted the stillness like a pebble tossed into a dark, mirrored pond. She waited, counting the seconds with her heart beats, listening to the remote, incessant surge and backwash of the sea.

Jennifer rang the bell again, pressing her face against the glass double doors. They were too fogged with dust and damp sea air to see anything but a blurred reflection of herself in the mirror of an old fashioned coat rack.

Perhaps the housekeeper was deaf, or out; or maybe when she had received Mr. Emmett's letter, she had simply packed her things and left Seacliff Pines altogether.

Jennifer twisted the knob. The door was locked. She stood for a few moments, listening to the quiet around her, when suddenly she had the weird sensation that she was being observed, the prickly feeling of eyes boring into her back. Turning quickly, she saw a large, gray cat sitting on the broad bannister; a mangy, emaciated cat, its eyes slitted in hostility. "Isn't anyone here?" Jennifer addressed the animal aloud. "Miss Collingwood might have at least left a note, a key..."

She turned back to the door. "Oh!" she exclaimed, startled.

A woman stood in the open doorway, a small woman of indeterminate age, with a pale, colorless face; the kind of face that might have belonged to an invalid confined for a very long time in a darkened, shade-drawn room.

"Miss... Miss Collingwood?"

24

The woman inclined her head slightly. She wore a dark green, shapeless dress relieved by a tiny white collar and a touch of white at the wrists.

"I'm Jennifer. Jennifer Sargent?"

Silently the woman stood aside. The hall which Jennifer stepped into was dark with wood paneling, thick with the odor of old carpets and mice. A tall grandfather clock ticked ponderously in one corner, its yellowed face dimmed by the shadow of a staircase.

"I'm Mrs. Kirkwood's great-niece," Jennifer said, raising her voice, thinking the woman might have a hearing problem.

The woman nodded, but did not speak. She kept staring at Jennifer, with deep set, hollowed eyes.

"Did you receive Mr. Emmett's letter?"

The thin bloodless lips remained sealed.

"Mr. Emmett said he would write and tell you..." Jennifer thought of the tilted mailbox outside the gate. Perhaps Mr. Emmett's letter, and hers too, were still there. "...I was coming. You *were* expecting me?"

"Yes." The word came out low and rusty as if Miss Collingwood was unaccustomed even to the briefest of verbal communication.

"I'm sorry, I couldn't give you the exact time of my arrival." Jennifer waited for Miss Collingwood's polite assurance that it was perfectly all right. None came. She began to feel more and more uncomfortable. "Mr. Emmett did explain why I'm here?"

"Yes," came the monosyllable spoken shallowly.

Jennifer thought that perhaps the housekeeper resented her. She would have to leave when the house was sold, and she resented that. But,

25

Jennifer remembered that Mr. Emmett had seemed to think Miss Collingwood was ready to retire. Perhaps the woman had relatives, a sister, a cousin, or a friend that she could plan to live with. And she did have the bequest.

"I hope you don't feel I'm turning you out." Jennifer said, forcing a smile.

"No."

Was she telling the truth? Another silence followed while Jennifer searched for something to say. She was conscious of the great, heavy doors, carved with fruits and flowers and cherubic faces, that were on either side of her. The clock tick-tocked, and somewhere above them a board creaked loudly.

Miss Collingwood lifted her head in frozen attention, her pale face stark in the dimness. The board creaked again, and a discernible shiver ran through the housekeeper's thin body. She turned large, frightened eyes on Jennifer.

"What is it?" Jennifer asked, a cold chill running down her spine.

"Don't you hear it?" Miss Collingwood whispered hoarsely.

"Hear what?" Jennifer asked, frightened, miserable, wanting desperately to pick up her suitcase and leave.

"Listen!" A thin finger went to her lips. "She's here. Mrs. Kirkwood. Upstairs. Walking."

"My aunt is dead," said Jennifer, the words not coming out as she had wanted them to in a firm, no-nonsense tone, but with a tremor and a squeak.

"She's come back," said Miss Collingwood, her hand at her throat. "She's come back from the dead. And she's walking upstairs."

CHAPTER III

Jennifer found herself trembling, and she was suddenly more afraid of showing her fear, more afraid of coming apart, than she was of whatever Miss Collingwood thought she had heard upstairs. Jennifer told herself that she mustn't listen to the old woman. She was obviously a little odd in the head. Jennifer knew better than to be pulled into that woman's crazy fantasies.

"I wonder..." Jennifer said, with what she thought was admirable control of her voice, "...I wonder if I could have a cup of coffee."

Miss Collingwood's eyes turned slowly on Jennifer. "Coffee?"

"Yes, I could use a cup." Jennifer smiled in encouragement, implying that coffee was just what Miss Collingwood needed too.

"In the kitchen," the housekeeper said, her voice rustling like grasshopper wings.

She turned and started down a passage under the stairs. Jennifer left her suitcase and followed, hurrying after her, down the dark length of the hall and through a door, coming into a high ceilinged kitchen. Curtains were drawn over the windows, and the light which filtered through was dim and uncertain. The kitchen had dreary paper covered walls, and a brown, faded teapot and tan cups and saucers were spread out on a bilious yellow tablecloth. There was a breakfast nook in an alcove, three benches and a round table. A cracked china clock on a shelf had stopped at twenty-past-two.

Miss Collingwood went to the stove and turned on a switch under a stained coffee pot.

"I'll just have it black," Jennifer said. "And, I'll get the cups."

Miss Collingwood motioned with her head in agreement. Jennifer went to the table and took two cups and saucers. "You'll join me?" Jennifer asked over her shoulder.

"I don't mind."

They sat at the round table. Jennifer had clicked on the overhead light as it was steadily getting darker; though her watch only said four-thirty. A peek through the curtains had revealed little to Jennifer except pine trees that looked like smeared blots of black-green in the fog which had crept in since her arrival.

"Is there a view of the ocean from the house?" Jennifer asked as Miss Collingwood wordlessly offered her the sugar bowl.

"No," she said, "too many trees."

The unsparing, overhead light exposed creases in Miss Collingwood's forehead that Jennifer hadn't noticed before. The light also revealed a fine webbing of wrinkles across her cheeks. Fifty-five? Sixty? Jennifer wondered about the woman's age.

"Had you been working for Aunt Hester a long time?" Jennifer asked, sipping at the bitter coffee.

"Thirty...thirty years," came the hesitant reply. Miss Collingwood's hair, a dull blonde streaked with gray, was worn in an untidy bun at

28

the nape of a thin, pipe-stem neck. Her face was small and homely, except for the eyes which might have been beautiful once. Now they simply stared out like round, wide windows in a white mask.

"And you've lived here all this time at Seacliff Pines?" Jennifer asked.

"Yes."

"You must be very attached to the house then." She made it half a question, hoping the housekeeper would say, "No," and that she was quite ready for a change.

But Miss Collingwood did not oblige. "It's..." She looked around her. "It's the only home I've known."

Guilt stirred in Jennifer's breast. "Have you made any plans?"

"No." She spoke to the curtained windows, her face impassive.

She isn't going to make it easy for me, Jennifer thought. "You have no friends, relatives?" she tried once more.

"No."

"I hate to put you out..." Jennifer began.

"I expected it," she said resignedly, without rancor.

"Mr. Emmett informed you that I was planning to sell the house?"

"Yes, I expected it. Mrs. Kirkwood always said whoever got it would sell it."

"Didn't she want it sold?"

A long pause. "I don't really know, Miss."

"Well," said Jennifer brightly, shaking her hair back, "maybe the people who buy it will keep you on."

Miss Collingwood's mournful eyes surveyed

Jennifer for a brief second. "Maybe." It was said in a neutral tone neither hopeful, nor unhopeful.

In the entry hall the grandfather clock whirred fussily, then bonged out the hour, five o-clock. The sound echoed eerily through the house, long after the clock had ceased to strike.

"Was my great-aunt very ill?" Jennifer inquired, breaking another silence.

"No. Not very."

Jennifer had the sudden impulse to scream. Miss Collingwood's voice, her inability to converse, to speak only when spoken to, had been subconsciously working like sandpaper in Jennifer's mind. "You were here when she died, weren't you?" Jennifer asked rather impatiently.

"Yes."

"Mr. Emmett said she died on May twelfth." Jennifer had never thought to ask for the specific cause of Hester's death, assuming that she was an old woman whose worn and aged body had simply given out.

Miss Collingwood stared down at her coffee cup, her thin, veined hands folded around it as if seeking warmth. "It...it stopped. Her heart stopped," she said in a sad whisper.

The drooping shoulders and the woebegone whisper pricked at Jennifer's conscience. "I'm sorry," she said in a softer tone. "I didn't mean to cross examine you. It's just that I..."

"It's all right," Miss Collingwood muttered.

"I want us to be friends," Jennifer said, reaching across impulsively and taking Miss Collingwood's hand. She felt the older woman's cold skin twitch as if in revulsion, but she ignored it and went on. "I know you may think me...well, self-centered, selfish, a stranger coming from nowhere wanting to sell Seacliff Pines." That the house was ugly in Jennifer's eyes did not shake her conviction of its salability. There were plenty of people in California, she had heard, who were drawn to oddities. "But you realize that I can't afford to live in it." She never would want to live in such a house. "And I want to assure you, I will do everything I can to see that you are comfortably situated before the new owners take possession."

"Thank you," said Miss Collingwood tonelessly.

"Well now, that's settled," said Jennifer smiling with counterfeit heartiness. "Is there a telephone here?"

"No."

John had been right. She wondered how Hester had managed without a phone.

"Do you shop for groceries at the general store in Torrey?" Jennifer asked.

"No. When... when Mrs. Kirkwood was alive, she went into San Francisco. There... there is a car out back in the garage."

"Does it run?" Mr. Emmett hadn't mentioned the car. Perhaps it had gone to Miss Collingwood as part of Hester's bequest.

"It... it did. I don't drive," she added.

Jennifer stared at her. "Then how did you..." eat, she wanted to say, "... get supplies?" Seven months alone in the house without a phone, unable to drive. No wonder the housekeeper seemed so thin, so gossamer-like.

"Oh... we... Mrs. Kirkwood got a big load of canned goods from some wholesale place before... before...." Her voice trailed off.

"May I see?"

Miss Collingwood got to her feet a little reluctantly. Crossing the kitchen, she opened a door, and Jennifer followed her into a large pantry. From the floor to the ceiling shelves were neatly stacked with off-brand cans of soup, vegetables, fruit and stews. Quite a few of the cans had lost their original labels and bore hand printed tapes describing their contents.

"My..." said Jennifer. "There's enough here to keep you for a long while."

"There's stacks more upstairs in the attic," Miss Collingwood volunteered.

"Upstairs?" Jennifer asked in surprise. So in addition to being thrifty, Aunt Hester had been a hoarder. Had she been afraid of going hungry? Jennifer's mother had had the same fear— baseless as it turned out—but Jennifer had grown up with intermittent, dire warnings of a growling wolf at the door. Perhaps that was why she had grasped so eagerly at her inheritance, wanting to wring every penny she could from it. Seacliff Pines, translated into cash, represented security, a material security she had never really known.

Turning from the pantry, Jennifer was on the verge of suggesting an inspection of the house when Miss Collingwood timidly offered to get supper. Being too excited Jennifer hadn't eaten much at lunch, and at Miss Collingwood's suggestion she suddenly discovered she was ravenous. She offered to help the housekeeper, and together they fixed a fairly edible meal from the stores of canned goods.

Again they sat in the nook. As nightfall deepened outside the curtained windows, Miss

Collingwood seemed to sink further into herself like a turtle folding into its shell. She ate little, and Jennifer had given up on conversation. She didn't know quite how to relate to the housekeeper. There was hardly much to relate *to*, since communication was so limited, and the woman's only revealed emotion was fear. Was Miss Collingwood really convinced her dead mistress haunted Seacliff Pines, or was she putting on an act, hoping to frighten Jennifer from the house? If the latter was true, the housekeeper was an extraordinary actress; a fact Jennifer very much doubted. That kind of fear, the quivering, the terrified eyes, the blanched face, had to be real.

When they had finished eating, Jennifer tactfully suggested, "Would you care to show me the rest of the house?"

Miss Collingwood started out of her reverie and turned shallow eyes on Jennifer. "The house . . . oh. In the morning? There . . . some of the rooms have no lights."

"No lights? Do you mean the electric bulbs have burned out?"

Miss Collingwood nodded in the affirmative.

Had there been no one to climb ladders to reach the overhead fixtures? Or was this another sign of Hester's frugality. No bulbs meant no lights, and that meant a smaller electric bill. Jennifer wondered what else was missing, broken, in need of replacement or repair. She had hoped the house would be in fairly good shape; in fact, she had counted on it since her funds were limited. Three hundred dollars was all she had now between her and complete poverty. It hadn't occurred to her that the house might require a good coat of paint on the outside, or that the grounds might be in need of a pruning back from its wild jungle state. These jobs would be costly and beyond her means.

Seacliff Pines would have to be sold as is, going for a few thousand less, a "fixer-upper" in real estate jargon. But there was still the five acres which went with it. And that must be worth something. She would see in the morning.

"Where do you suggest I sleep tonight?" Jennifer asked.

"Upstairs," Miss Collingwood said. "There are six bedrooms upstairs. Three above that."

"Any particular bedroom?"

Miss Collingwood took a few seconds before she answered. "I sleep downstairs. Down the hall from the kitchen."

"Are the beds made up?"

"No. I can't use the stairs. My back." She pressed one hand to the small of her back, but Jennifer had the feeling that Miss Collingwood's reluctance to climb the stairs had little to do with her back.

"If you will give me linens, I'll be glad to make up my own bed."

Miss Collingwood went out into the hall with Jennifer at her heels. From a closet behind the stairs she took out folded white sheets, pillow cases, and a blanket smelling of moth balls. She piled them into Jennifer's outstretched arms.

"Thank you, Miss Collingwood. And good night."

As Jennifer climbed the stairs, she was conscious of the housekeeper's stare. At the top, Jennifer turned. Miss Collingwood was watching her, one pale hand on the newel, the other at her throat. Although her face was in shadow, it seemed to Jennifer that the woman stood there with an air of expectancy.

"It's quite dark up here," Jennifer said.

The housekeeper moved to the wall, and Jennifer heard the sound of a click. A dim circle of light blossomed over her head. "There's a switch up there, too," Miss Collingwood offered.

From where Jennifer stood on the wide landing she could see a fan shaped, stained glass window. Beneath it was a green stone urn holding a single, drooping peacock feather.

"You needn't wait," Jennifer said. "I'll be all right."

Miss Collingwood moved her lips soundlessly, then slowly moved away from the wall and with one last upward glance at Jennifer, disappeared under the stairs.

Jennifer picked a door at random, the second from the top of the stairs. It was a fair sized room, tidy, smelling of dust and mildew, unimaginatively dull in its furnishings. Apparently it was once a pink and gold room. But now the colors were faded; the gold sprigged wallpaper, the heavy curtains, the pink bedspread and figured rug had been worn to lusterless hues by time. A murky reproduction of a dispirited Indian on horseback looked down from the wall above the bed. Beyond the bureau Jennifer saw the edge of a bathtub through a half-open door. It was not the sort of accommodations to cheer one after a long, tiresome day, but Jennifer was grateful for anything of passing comfort. And her first view of the house had promised far less.

After she made up her bed, she went down to fetch her suitcase from the entry hall where she had left it hours earlier. Except for the loud ticking of the clock the house was very still. The glass doors threw back her reflected image, and turning, she contemplated herself in the mirror: a white-faced girl with long, dark hair and large eyes which looked—scared?

She hurried up the stairs, hesitated and decided to leave the light on. The door to the bedroom was open; although she thought she had closed it. She shut it firmly now, unpacked her night things and got ready for bed. She wondered if Miss Collingwood slept with her door locked and the covers up over her head. Jennifer glanced at the door. There was no key, but why should she need one? She wasn't Miss Collingwood.

She got into bed, read for awhile, and growing tired, she switched off the light. Darkness closed over her, breathless with the stuffy odor of moth balls from the blanket. She wondered if she ought to get up and open the window, but instead she settled herself more comfortably on the pillows.

Suddenly, a wheezing groan made her sit bolt upright. Her eyes stared out of their sockets as a cold current of air touched the back of her neck. She turned her head slowly and saw that the door had opened. Her heart began to beat painfully in her chest.

"Miss Collingwood?" Her voice seemed an affront in the heavy silence.

Hinges rasped as the door, opening to its full width, thumped against the inner wall. Jennifer's damp fingers clutched at the blankets as she craned her neck forward. "Miss Collingwood?" she whispered. She waited, waited it seemed for long minutes for someone, a shadow, anything to cross the threshhold. But she saw nothing, only a corner of dimly lit carpet in the hallway.

Gradually she let out her breath, her heart slowed its pace. "Really! Talk about Miss Collingwood! A door opens and I nearly jump out of my skin. The door probably has a faulty catch, or perhaps it is hung all wrong and refuses to stay shut unless it is closed in a special way." Jennifer spoke to herself, trying to calm her rattled nerves.

She got out of bed and examined the knob and catch, then carefully pressed the door shut. The moment her back was turned, it creaked open again. Irritated, she went back and as she was inspecting the door again, she heard a series of sounds in the corridor, tinkling, jingling sounds.

At that sound her mind went swiftly back through the years, back to a cafe on Randolph Street where as a child she had sat in rapt attention, listening to a woman with rouged cheeks, a woman who, as she talked, kept fidgeting with a row of brassy gold bracelets on her arm. And they had made that same tinkle, that same, soft, delicate jingle.

Perhaps, Jennifer thought, ice forming around her heart, Miss Collingwood was right after all. Perhaps Aunt Hester's ghost did walk the upper regions of Seacliff Pines.

CHAPTER IV

When Jennifer awoke the next morning, the first thing she saw was the chair she had jammed under the door knob to keep the door closed. A band of sunlight had worked its way through a gap in the curtains, wrapping itself about the chair's curved, slatted back. Jennifer determined to get a key as she sat watching the moving, gilded dust motes. She didn't like doors opening all by themselves.

She thought of the jingling sound she had heard and quickly jumped out of bed. She went to the window and pulled aside the curtains. Fog still lingered in thin patches among the lower branches of the trees where the sun had not yet reached. She opened the window, and the sound of the ocean became louder, the incessant, ever present boom of the restless surf.

Directly below her were masses of overgrown shrubbery, and when she turned her head, she could see a paved terrace littered with pine needles and the silvery green leaves of a tall eucalyptus. A crumbling, stone carved wall enclosed the terrace. In one corner a large terra cotta pot held a desiccated geranium. A gull landed on the stone balustrade. Cocking its head, he looked up toward the house, then with a sudden frightened squawk and a rustle of wings, flew off. Jennifer hugged her

38

arms against the chill. Even the birds seemed frightened of the house.

She turned and surveyed the room, infinitely more shabby in the light of day. She was surprised to find that it was just an ordinary dingy room in an ugly house. There was nothing to be afraid of. Besides, fear was a luxury she could not afford. She couldn't give a convincing sales pitch to a prospective buyer if she acted as if she were scared of her own shadow. As for Aunt Hester haunting the place that was just something in Miss Collingwood's mind, something which Jennifer's own subconscious had taken up and played upon after a tired, exhausting day. The house groaned and squeaked and jingled because it was an old house. The sea damp swelled the wooden boards; the warmth of the day contracted them. Ill fitting doors and mice perhaps scurrying about could also be causes of noise. All sorts of things could be explained logically without having to pop one's eyes and yell "ghost!"

She wasn't going to allow her stay at Seacliff Pines to be marred by ghost stories, or by gloom. She cheered up suddenly remembering John McGraw, his warm smile and friendly eyes. How quickly they had become friends, as if they had known one another for years. And he was close by, only a half-mile away, a neighbor. Tonight she would see him, and in her mind she began to compose an amusing account of her first night at Seacliff Pines: Miss Collingwood's spooky voice and frightened eyes, the door that wouldn't stay closed, and how she had gone all goose-pimply because a current of air had caught some beaded lamp and made it jingle.

Feeling more cheerful, she got dressed and went downstairs. Miss Collingwood was filling the coffee pot at the sink. "Good morning," Jennifer said, smiling.

Miss Collingwood returned Jennifer's smile with a pale one of her own. "Good morning."

Jennifer hoped that that smile was a good omen. Perhaps the housekeeper had lost her shyness. She wanted Miss Collingwood to like her, to ease the niggling guilt she felt about forcing her from Seacliff Pines. Above all Jennifer, whose childhood had been filled with her mother's penchant for crises, wanted things to go smoothly and easily.

They had stale cornflakes and canned milk for breakfast. The sun, slanting diagonally down from the trees outside, threw fingers of custard-colored light across the window sill. Jennifer said: "It looks like a lovely day, doesn't it?"

"Yes," said Miss Collingwood.

She wanted to inquire where her great-aunt had been buried. She thought it only fitting that she visit her benefactor's grave and lay a wreath on it, or at the least a bouquet of flowers. The old woman had died alone, without friends, unmourned except for Miss Collingwood. So, although it was obvious that the topic of Hester's death disturbed the housekeeper, Jennifer felt that there were some things she ought to know.

Miss Collingwood was returning the canned milk to the refrigerator when Jennifer took the bull by the horns. "Could you tell me where the Kirkwoods are buried?"

Miss Collingwood mumbled something inaudibly, and Jennifer said, "Pardon?"

Miss Collingwood, her hand at her throat,

40

turned and looked at Jennifer. "They're not buried," she said hoarsely.

Oh, Lordy, Jennifer thought, here we go again. The ghost and the walking dead bit. "I don't believe in ghosts," Jennifer said firmly, feeling that her words were falling on strongly opinionated ears.

She was right. "*I* do," said Miss Collingwood. "And if you had ever seen one, you would too."

It was useless to argue. "Maybe," Jennifer commented and left it at that.

Miss Collingwood had gone back to poking about in the refrigerator, and when she was through, Jennifer said, "I was told the grounds cover five acres. Is there a fence around the property?"

Miss Collingwood thought for a moment. "Yes—I believe there is."

Jennifer finished her coffee and wondered whether she should inspect the house first or take a look outside. Five acres was a lot of looking. She decided to take just a peek, and a kind of excitement took hold, the same excitement she had experienced on the plane ride from Chicago when she felt important because she owned a house. For the first time in her life she had something of her own besides the clothing on her back and a ten year old, dilapidated car. It gave her a secure feeling, a flush feeling like a small boy whose pockets were suddenly jingling with coins.

"I think I'll have a look outside," she said through the pantry door to Miss Collingwood.

The last bit of fog had disappeared from under the trees, but the ground was still damp, and when

41

the branches shivered in the small breeze, drops fell from the glistening leaves. Jennifer walked slowly around the house. If there had ever been any kind of formal garden, Jennifer saw no indication of it. It seemed that Aunt Hester had simply allowed whichever plant, shrub or tree had taken root to flourish without check. All types of evergreens, firs, great lofty crowned redwoods, deodars spreading wide arms and gloomy cypress crowded close to the house. Someone long ago must have put in nasturtiums, but now they ran wild, climbing trees and shrubs, hanging in festoons from the branches. Pale, star jasmine peeped out from the hardier, creeping periwinkle, their scent mingling with the resinous pine and salt sea air.

Jennifer found a moss-streaked path which seemed to lead in the direction of the sea. She took it, brushing aside the wet dripping branches which sprang back in a shower of drops as she passed. A minute later when she turned to look at the house, it had disappeared from view.

A soft wind sighed in the trees and then fell silent. High above, somewhere amid the leafed and needled branches, a dove mourned sad and forlorn. Thin shafts of watery sunlight slanted down through the trees, light that did not light but only seemed to make the surrounding dark look heavier.

Somehow Jennifer did not feel comfortable in the wild, jungle setting. In fact a strange uneasiness had gripped her, and when a twig snapped, she wheeled about, her heart beating erratically. She felt oppressed, trapped, as if she had been lured into the forest by something or someone who meant her harm. It was an absurd sensation, totally unreasonable. She was not lost. She had only to retrace her steps, and in a matter of minutes she would be back in sunlight. But the anxious feeling persisted; yet, she would not give in to it. She would not go back. She hurried along, dread nipping at her heels, until at last she emerged from the trees aware that she had been holding her breath for some time. She stood a few moments taking in great gulps of air as if she had been wildly running from the dark, tangled, reed choked forest behind her.

She wondered at what had come over her. Fear of the house, fear of the woods and her crazy imagination, feeling eyes at her back and hearing jingling bracelets, made her feel foolish. "Really," she told herself, "I'm acting like a nit-wit, not like Jennifer Sargent at all."

Calmer now, she looked around and found herself on a plateau covered with tall, yellow grass rippling in the breeze. She continued on the path to the edge of the cliff. From there it was a sheer drop to the black rocks below, where the water curled and broke in bursts of white spray. To the left of the rocks was a tiny crescent of pale, sandy beach. Jennifer, walking along the cliff's edge and seeking a way down, could find none except by a hazardous descent where the cliff fell in slightly less precipitous fashion. It was another disappointment. She couldn't honestly advertise the house as having easy access to a beach, a factor which might have mitigated its ugly appearance.

As she continued her walk, her expectations continued to diminish. What she had thought, at first sight, to be a wide, flat plateau was in reality a long, narrow one broken up by several boulder strewn canyons and gullies, deep gaps in the ground eroded by long dried up rivers which had once found their meandering way through here to the sea. In all probability, except for the woods, the builders of Seacliff Pines had taken advantage of the only feasible building site on the entire five acres. Of course she knew houses were sometimes built on stilts, artificial foundations erected on the most unlikeliest of sites, but even so, the Kirkwood chopped-up acreage would fetch a lot less than she had hoped for. Perhaps she would have to sell the house and grounds all of one piece.

Jennifer retraced her steps back through the trees, forcing herself to stroll. Her panicky fear of the dark, entangled forest was gone, but an undercurrent of discomfort remained. She recognized it now as a feeling akin to the one she had experienced the day she walked along the marble-floored corridor to Mr. Emmett's office. She had a lost feeling, a feeling of unknown dread even then, and now it had come back to her.

When she reached the drive, she was pleasantly surprised to find John McGraw sitting on the front steps.

"Ah—there you are," he said, getting to his feet. "The housekeeper said you had gone out for a walk."

"Wouldn't she let you in?" Jennifer asked.

"She didn't invite me, if that's what you mean. And I didn't press it."

"I think she's afraid of strangers," Jennifer said. They went up the stairs together.

"She did look at me as if I were a four-headed monster," John remarked.

"In fact, she's afraid, period. She thinks my

great-aunt is haunting the house," Jennifer smiled.

"Is she?"

For a moment Jennifer stared at John, then realizing he was pulling her leg, she said, "Of course. She appears every night at the stroke of twelve in bedroom slippers and baby blue, see-through pajamas."

They both laughed.

The door was locked, and Jennifer rang the bell. "I've forgotten to ask for a key," she told John while they were waiting. "What brings you here so early? Not that I'm sorry to see you, but our date was for this evening."

"I know. But I'd clean forgotten the appointment I had tonight, an appointment with this man who's coming down to talk about some property. So, I thought I'd come over and invite you for lunch instead. At my place. How about it?"

"Well...I haven't looked the house over yet..."

"It can wait. Come on. I want you to see where I live."

"All right, then. Let me change my shoes." She jabbed at the bell again, and a moment later Miss Collingwood opened the door. Her pale face was stained pink as if she had hurried.

"I'm sorry," Jennifer said. "This is John McGraw—a neighbor."

Miss Collingwood gave John a quick glance and muttered something inaudible.

"Wait down here," Jennifer told John. "I'll only be a minute."

She ran up to her room, glad that John had come, but thinking that even his presence downstairs, solid and reassuring as it was, did not dispel the dark, oppressive dreariness of the house. The shadows of Seacliff Pines seemed to have swallowed him up the moment he crossed the threshold, just as they had swallowed her.

She changed hurriedly from her damp sandals into a pair of dry loafers. Hastily pulling a comb through her long hair she flung one last look at herself in the mirror. She looked pink-cheeked and happy, so different an image than the one of last night. Perhaps she was being overdramatic about the house. "Swallowing shadows. Really!" She reprimanded herself.

She let herself out, closing the door, waiting for a moment to see if it would spring open. When it did not she shrugged. She thought it funny that none of the other doors along the corridor seemed to behave so oddly.

When she got back to the entry hall John was not there. She looked out on the veranda, thinking he might have stepped out for a breath of air, or had decided to wait in his car. But he was nowhere to be seen. Perhaps he was taking a stroll. Then suddenly remembering her lack of a key, she went to look for Miss Collingwood.

She found her in the kitchen, sitting at the breakfast table, polishing silver. Jennifer asked for a key, explaining that she was going out to lunch with John McGraw. "I don't know when I'll be back," she said. "Surely before dark."

There seemed to be a sudden relief in Miss Collingwood's eyes at the mention of returning before dark, but Jennifer couldn't tell for sure. The ghost Miss Collingwood feared walked at night, and perhaps she was glad of any company, once the sun set; any company, that is, who was alive, breathing and sane. Even Jennifer, who one day soon was going to sell the roof over her head, was welcome. How terrible it must be to fear a place so much and to have to remain there because there was nowhere else to go.

"There's a set of keys in my room," Miss Collingwood said.

Jennifer followed her out of the kitchen along a dark passage to what seemed the very bowels of the house. Miss Collingwood stopped before a door, hesitated, then turned to Jennifer. "If you'll wait…" she said in her low, hoarse voice. She opened the door a crack and slid through.

Jennifer wondered why Miss Collingwood was so secretive. Had she something hidden in her room, something which she would rather not have anyone see? Jennifer thought it unlikely. Miss Collingwood's secretiveness went with her personality, the fluttering hand to the throat, the shyness, the fear.

A few minutes later the housekeeper slipped out and handed Jennifer a large bunch of keys on a brass ring. "I'm not taking all your keys, am I?" Jennifer asked.

"It doesn't matter. I never go out."

"Thank you, then."

When Jennifer returned to the front hall, John was sitting on the wide bench of the clothes rack. "I was walking around outside," he explained, getting to his feet and taking her arm.

"What do you think?" she asked.

"Of the house? To be truthful, what I've seen of it doesn't exactly bowl me over. It's not my type.

47

But then you'd be surprised how many people go in for Victoriana. What's the rest of it like?" He opened the door, and they went out.

"I told you; I haven't seen it yet."

"Oh yes. Well, it doesn't matter. The strong selling point is the location—the acreage."

"I'm afraid the acreage won't help much either." She explained why.

He helped her into the car. "Still, you ought to get a good price."

"How good?"

"You can begin at one hundred thousand."

"That's ridiculous!" She laughed.

"You never know," he said closing the door. He came around and got in behind the wheel. "Some well-off, retired couple from Iowa might take one look at it and claim it's their dream house."

"I hope so—but one hundred thousand dollars?" She shook her head.

John's house, a small white cottage with green shutters, was situated well back from the road, like Seacliff Pines and the other homes in the area. However, except for one lone pepper tree which shaded the roof, it stood open to the sun and as a consequence had a superb view of the Pacific.

"Not bad for a rental at eighty dollars a month, is it?" John asked, inserting a key in the lock. From the other side of the door Rena began to bark.

"Fantastic," said Jennifer.

John opened the door, and a huge bundle of white hair leaped at him, nearly knocking him backward. "Down, Rena! Down, I say!" She obeyed, her pink tongue licking John's shoes; her whole body wagging and whimpering with love.

"You'd think I'd been away for a month," said John over his shoulder. "Come in, come in."

The cottage had one large room and a tiny kitchen. There were bookshelves and bright cushions on the sofa, a work bench in one corner and a potter's wheel. "It's not a palace," said John apologetically.

"I think it's great," said Jennifer, looking around. "It's certainly far more attractive—more homey—than Seacliff Pines."

John had fixed a casserole that he called turkey supreme, and it was surprisingly good. With it they had a salad and a bottle of white wine. "You are a marvelous cook," said Jennifer appreciatively, a picture of the rows and rows of canned goods at the Pines rising before her. "I'd trade you for Miss Collingwood any day."

He smiled and reaching across the table, squeezed her hand.

John was a good listener, easy to talk to, easy to be with. He and Jennifer were soon telling each other about their pasts. He was from a small town in Missouri, had gone to college, and then had worked in his uncle's real estate office until a year ago; when fed up with the business, he had quit and come to Torrey. "I always wanted to be creative," he said, "I'm not the best potter in the world, but it's fun."

After lunch, with Rena tagging at their heels, they descended a wooden staircase to the beach; a tawny, sanded inlet where the breaking waves reached for their bare feet with fingers of foam. Sandpipers on black toothpick legs, skittered along the edge of the tide, pecking busily at the

49

hard packed sand. As they walked, a flock of gulls rose before them in noisy confusion and wheeled out to sea.

Jennifer took a long, deep breath of the windy, sea air. She was happy and full of optimism now that she had put some distance between herself and the Pines. "You know what I would like to do?" she asked John. "Travel. I want to see the whole wide world." She threw her arms out.

"Not me," said John, slipping his arm through hers. "I'd like to make a wad of dough and build a fantastic house with every gadget in it known to man—and just sit in it—never having to work a day in my life again."

"Work," said Jennifer scornfully. "You don't know what work is until you've had to slave for someone like Mr. Goodbody."

"I've had my share of Goodbodys too," he said soberly.

They came to a tiny headland of jutting rocks, the dog trotting on ahead of them. Suddenly, galvinized by the sight of a gull preening on the tallest of the stone projections, Rena scrambled across the rocks, jumping for the bird a moment before it took off, and barking at it crazily as it flew away.

Together, Jennifer and John climbed over the rocks and little pools that had been left by the outgoing tide, teemed with sea life, tiny crabs, strange, vermillion flowering creatures, anemones, and a baby, transparent purple jelly fish. On the other side was another beach, and Jennifer looking up at the cliff exclaimed, "Aren't we below Seacliff Pines?"

"I guess we are," said John. "I told you it was only a half-mile away."

"I wish there was some way to get down to the beach from above."

"Isn't there?"

"Not that I could find." Her eyes scanned the side of the steep bluff, spotted with clumps of pale yellow flowering shrubs. "I guess the Kirkwoods didn't go in for swimming, or sunning either." They walked a few more paces when Jennifer pointed. "Look, aren't those steps?"

A crude staircase, parts of it almost completely hidden by overhanging ice plants, went up the side of the cliff. The steps were made of stones and shells mortared together with clay.

"I'm going to try to climb it," said Jennifer, delighted.

"No," said John, his hand on her arm. "I don't think you'd better. It's a steep climb, and those crazy stairs don't look safe."

"Well...." she said reluctantly. "Maybe you're right."

It was close to four, and the fog was already creeping up the drive when John drove Jennifer back to the house. "That was fun," John said. He leaned over and kissed her lightly on the cheek. "Let's do it again."

"Yes, let's."

She liked John. He was not the most exciting person in the world, but she liked him. He was comfortable to be with, and he was a nice person, a nice man.

"Maybe, I'll drop by tomorrow," he said, "in case you need a lift into town."

"Oh. Miss Collingwood said that there's a car here, in the garage. I have no idea what it's like or even if it will start."

"Let me have a look," he said, getting out of the car.

"Won't it make you late?"

"Not very."

The garage at the back was a miniature copy of the house, gabled and frescoed, with brown peeling paint. From the outside it appeared to be a good sized building, but when John opened the doors (surprisingly unlocked), the interior proved to be barely large enough to house two cars. There was one there now, a Pontiac of so ancient a vintage that Jennifer could not even begin to guess its year.

"Fifty-five," John said. "Looks in pretty good shape. Do you have a key?"

Jennifer, trying a number of keys on her ring, found the right one, but the car wouldn't start.

"The battery's probably dead," John said. "I'll take it with me and have it charged."

"John, really..."

"No trouble," he said.

He got some tools from the trunk of his car and removed the battery. "You're really very neighborly, you know," she said.

"It isn't hard with a neighbor like you," he smiled.

Later when John drove off, Jennifer stood in the drive for a few moments, feeling curiously abandoned and depressed. The fog, shrouding the treetops, was beginning to sift downward, opaque, milky and cold. With an involuntary shudder she returned to the house.

Within the house dusk had come. Gray light filtered through the glass doors in two, long rectangles on the faded hall carpet, and beyond them was the shadowy staircase disappearing upward into darkness.

Jennifer flicked the light switch, but nothing happened. Puzzled, she turned and felt along the corridor to the kitchen. When she pushed the door open, the weird brilliance of candlelight greeted her. There were flickering candles on the stove and refrigerator, on the counters and on shelves. There were fat, waxy candles and tall, slim tapers; some of them set in holders, others in saucers. Hearing Jennifer, Miss Collingwood turned with a start from lighting a five-pronged candelabra; her eyes were large and luminous, reflecting pinpoints of flame.

"Lights go out?" Jennifer asked.

"The fuse...I...I blew a fuse when I plugged in the iron."

"Aren't there other fuses? Replacements, I mean."

"No," she said. "We're out."

Jennifer sighed. She ought to have gone shopping. "I'll have to put that on my list, then, and try to get to the store tomorrow."

Miss Collingwood went back to lighting candles.

Jennifer stared at the housekeeper's back, eloquent with silence like the blank, closed doors upstairs.

"I think I'll have a look at the ground floor before supper," Jennifer said suddenly.

Miss Collingwood turned. "But the lights..."

"It won't matter. I'll use candles. You needn't

come," she added. "I'm sure I won't get lost." She
had to do something. She had no desire to sit in the
kitchen, trying to make conversation with Miss
Collingwood. "Do you mind if I take the candelabra?"

"No...no...I..." She paused, her eyes shifting
to the door, and Jennifer waited for her to go on.
"Supper will be ready by six," she finally said.

Jennifer had the odd feeling that Miss Collingwood had been on the verge of telling her
something, something more important than announcing supper at six.

"I won't be far away," Jennifer said.

Armed with the heavy candelabra and accompanied by her leaping shadow grotesquely thrown
against the heavy wood paneling of the passage,
Jennifer made her way to the entry hall. She had
decided to start at the front of the house, a logical
beginning. Opening the carved double doors to the
right of the entrance, she came into a large, high
ceilinged room, the windows curtained by a sweep
of tasseled brocade. The wavering light from the
candles flickered off the gilt in the wallpaper and
revealed tufted, uncomfortable looking chairs, a
love seat with a carved back, a maroon velvet sofa,
tables crowded with bric-a-brac, boxes and trays
and wax roses under glass. From a deep, shadowed
corner a life-sized statue of a Nubian girl smiled
fatuously. Everything smelled of upholstery rot
and thick layers of dust.

A portrait of a woman over the narrow, tiled
fireplace caught her eye, and moving closer she
recognized it as a younger version of Hester
Kirkwood. Apparently she had posed for the
picture in the costume of Cleopatra, long black

wig, beaded headress, the eyes penciled black and heavily shadowed. Except for the resolute set of the chin—which the artist had either been unable or unwilling to disguise—Hester must have been a very attractive woman.

Jennifer turned and surveyed the room again. Trailing a finger along a table velvety with dust, Jennifer thought that this was the sort of place that a retired couple from Iowa would delight in.

Peering into the room directly across the hall, Jennifer noted the floor-to-ceiling shelves of books and guessed that it was the library. Unlike the parlor, it had a fresh, pleasant smell, the smell of lemon furniture polish. From the way the heavy cumbersome desk and the dark mahogany gleamed, it was apparent that this was one room Miss Collingwood still kept up. Facing the fireplace were two huge wing back chairs; and when Jennifer lifted her candles for a better view, she saw that here, too, above the mantel, was a large portrait. She went over to it, and setting the candelabra down, studied the picture. It was of a man in his forties with a bushy, light brown moustache, brown, wavy hair and very blue and very amused eyes. "Hubert Kirkwood," the plaque at the bottom said.

This was Uncle Hubert. He was a distinguished looking man—aquiline nose, firm chin. The mouth, interesting in its way, saved him from slick, picture-ad handsomeness. It was a wide, rather sensuous mouth, and Jennifer wondered if he had loved Aunt Hester as much as Hester had said she loved him.

Suddenly Jennifer was jolted out of her contemplation by the sound of the door creaking behind her, and as it banged shut, the candles began to waver dangerously.

"Oh, no!" she exclaimed as three of them blew out. With a shaking hand, Jennifer relit them, and shadows leaped into life again, dancing strangely above her head. She stared at the flames, burning with a steady incandescence, and as she stared, she began to have the eerie feeling that she was not alone in the room.

Jennifer wondered if Miss Collingwood had silently followed her, and had closed the door. She had only to turn her head to see, but her head refused to obey.

Her heart began to beat loudly as she battled the old feeling of entrapment. She worried if her mind was slipping. Was she really claustrophobic? Or was it just Seacliff Pines? She didn't know, and she didn't care. She had to get out of the room.

She steadied herself, leaning her head against the cool mantel for a few moments; then, taking a deep breath, she picked up the candelabra.

She turned and a pulse jumped in her throat as she found herself staring into the very blue eyes of a man seated in one of the wing chairs. The nose, the mouth, the light brown moustache—it was Uncle Hubert! For a fraction of a second horror gagged her. Then she found her voice and screamed.

CHAPTER V

Later, when she thought of her screaming panic, it seemed nothing short of a miracle that she had not dropped the candelabra as she stumbled blindly across the room, wrestled with the door and rushed out into the corridor, where she nearly collided with Miss Collingwood. But she had held grimly on to it, and now, as she leaned with her back against the wall, trying to control her shaking limbs, the candle flames winked and blinked illuminating in their uncertain light, the housekeeper's white, oval face.

"What is it?" Miss Collingwood asked hoarsely of Jennifer, her hands twitching at the sides of her skirt.

Jennifer shook her head. "There...in there..." She swallowed and took a deep breath. "There's a man...sitting...in the chair..."

"Oh," said Miss Collingwood with relief. "*That*. That's Mr. Kirkwood."

Jennifer stared at her. "No...you must be mistaken. He *looks* like him. Mr. Kirkwood is dead."

"Yes. He died. It will be thirty years in December. December fifth. And he's been sitting there ever since."

"But...it can't be." Jennifer felt as if reality had somehow slipped through her fingers. "That

57

man...is *not* a ghost." She would not believe in ghosts. Wild horses could drag her through the woods and down to the beach, but she would not let her mind accept the supernatural. "It can't be his corpse..."

"He's stuffed," said Miss Collingwood.

"*What?*"

"He's stuffed. Like a bird or a fish. They take out the insides and give them glass eyes."

"Disgusting," said Jennifer, pushing the candelabra into Miss Collingwood's hands. She had to sit down somewhere, anywhere; her knees were like water. And her stomach—she felt sick.

The clothes rack was nearest, and she lowered herself on the hard, slippery bench. "It's too awful, barbaric," she shuddered. "Isn't there some kind of law against that sort of thing?"

"I don't know," said Miss Collingwood.

"But...when people die, they're *buried*," she argued, still shocked.

"Mr. Kirkwood's remains—I mean, what was left over was buried, I suppose."

"And my great-aunt had him...him stuffed? Why?"

"She loved him," said Miss Collingwood simply.

"But it isn't...it isn't *natural*."

Miss Collingwood seemed to ponder on that a moment or two. "You get used to him. He doesn't hurt anybody sitting there in his favorite chair." And then, she added in a wistful voice. "Mr. Kirkwood was a wonderful man. I keep the library for him. He liked to sit there in front of the fire." Taking the candles, she turned and walked into the library.

Jennifer got to her feet and followed still

protesting. "But there was nothing in the will that said he shouldn't be buried."

"I don't know about the will," Miss Collingwood said with an undercurrent of obstinacy in her voice that startled Jennifer. It was the first time the housekeeper had shown anything but meekness or fear.

"Didn't Mrs. Kirkwood say anything to you about disposing of the body in the event of her death?" Jennifer asked.

"No." The housekeeper stood with her back to the fireplace, gazing at Hubert Kirkwood.

Jennifer forced herself to look at him again. The skin, she noticed now that she had a more dispassionate view, sagged in yellow folds like wrinkled parchment; an embalmed smile was drawn back from yellowed teeth, and the glassy eyes stared back at her in unflinching blue. Despite all, Hubert Kirkwood still looked very life-like. It was so macabre!

She had no stomach for further exploration—or for supper—and she excused herself to Miss Collingwood and went to bed. The housekeeper had found an old, oil lamp for Jennifer, and once in bed she tried to read by it; but the amber flame was too feeble, and her concentration poor. She thought back to her exuberance when she had first learned she had inherited Seacliff Pines, her one chance to escape from a dull life. "No complications," Mr. Emmett had said.

But, of course, the old lawyer had never seen the unsightly house or its botched acreage or Miss Collingwood. And obviously he was unaware of Uncle Hubert. Uncle Hubert. She would have to bury him, no matter if it did make Hester turn over in her grave. That meant another unavoidable expense. It was a hard, maybe mercenary, way to look at it, but the house had been left outright (no strings attached), to an heir, herself, and Mr. Emmett had practically assured her she could do with it as she pleased. That included disposing of everything as she saw fit, furniture, grounds and stuffed corpses as well.

So rationalizing, she fell asleep. Once, when she awoke in the restless still of the night, she lay in the darkness listening a long time to the house's queer noises, the creakings and groanings, the wind howling through the firs outside. Again she had the strange sensation that Miss Collingwood might be right, that somewhere in the house Hester's spirit kept watch. But why Hester's and not Hubert's? Had Hester left some unfinished business, something important behind when she died? Was Hester the stronger willed of the two, so strong willed she could cross over from the dead?

"I don't believe that," Jennifer told herself, staring blindly at the ceiling. "I must not allow myself to believe it. The dead stay dead. It's the house, the dark, dim corridors, the heavy carvings, the curtained windows, that puts these ideas into my head. There's something evil in the air." And her last thought before sinking into sleep was, "Maybe I shouldn't have come."

When morning came and she opened her eyes to a room unexpectedly radiant with sunshine, she shoved her doubts, her pessimism aside. Beyond the window between the nodding fir tree branches, the sky was a pure, undiluted blue. She jumped out of bed, touched her toes, counting, one, two, three, up to ten; did several knee bends; opened the window and took a deep breath of cold, brisk air.

Today, she refused to have one gloomy thought. She would keep busy; there was so much to do, sweeping and polishing, cleaning windows, sorting over the bric-a-brac. Later, when John brought the car's battery, she would go into Torrey. She would buy fresh vegetables, fruit, milk and fuses. She would telephone one of the San Francisco papers and put an ad in for the house, and the sooner the better. Her ownership of the house was a sure thing, and by the time the estate was settled, hopefully any day, she might have a buyer lined up. And, she thought as she dressed in a pair of navy pants, she would try to have a telephone installed. Yes, it might be an extravagance, and John had told her they were hard to come by, but if prospective buyers wanted to contact her, she would need one. (She did not want to admit to herself that a telephone would also make her feel safe because she did not know exactly what she ought to feel safe *from*.)

Jennifer's brisk cheerfulness survived the silence of Miss Collingwood at breakfast, and the quiet torpid chill of the downstairs rooms. Jennifer remained in good spirits while she went from room to room, changing yellowed covers from furniture and opening windows to freshen the stale, heavy air. Everywhere dust lay thick like plush velvet, and cobwebs hung like gray gossamer cocoons. The rooms were jammed with turn-of-the-century furniture, pictures, statues, beaded lamps, purple velour footstools, sofas and gilt framed chairs. It was as if the Kirkwoods had raided every Victorian house in the country, hauling these treasures—or what they believed to be treasures—back to Seacliff Pines.

Shortly before noon Jennifer was interrupted in

her sweeping and dusting by John McGraw. He had come to install her recharged battery.

"How are things going?" he asked Jennifer as she sat on an overturned box in the garage and watched him.

"Oh, all right, I guess, except for..." and she told him about Hubert.

John whistled in astonishment. "I can't believe it," he said.

"Don't you think I ought to ask Mr. Emmett's advice before I do anything with him?" Jennifer asked.

"Why? Just have him buried or cremated."

"That's what I thought too."

He banged the hood of the old Pontiac down and wiped his hands on a rag. "I've been passing the word along," John said, "about the house. You might get a couple of bites."

"You don't think it's too soon? I haven't got clear title yet."

"Doesn't hurt. I think she'll run now. Got the key? Let me give her a try."

The engine heaved and grunted like a giant in the throes of some mysterious ailment. Then with a sudden, explosive cough the motor caught and settled into a steady, rackety rhythm.

"I don't know how to thank you," Jennifer said, as John got out of the car. "Won't you stay for lunch?"

"Can't. I left some pitchers and cups in the kiln, and I've got to get back. I'll take a rain-check, though."

"Okay. That's a promise."

After a quick sandwich Jennifer gathered all her cleaning apparatus together and went upstairs. The first door she tried, the one directly across the hall from hers, was locked. Surprised, Jennifer fetched her keys and inserting each one in turn, found that none of them seemed to fit. She ran quickly down the stairs.

"Miss Collingwood," she said to the housekeeper who was coming out of the library. "There's a door upstairs that's locked."

Miss Collingwood stared at Jennifer, her face pale and expressionless like a suspended white oval mask against the sepia gloom of the hall.

"The bedroom upstairs," Jennifer repeated. "The one across the hall from mine."

Miss Collingwood's eyes seemed to grow larger. "None of the bedrooms are locked," she whispered. "That's..." Her mouth trembled, and she put her fingers to it.

"Never mind," said Jennifer impatiently. "Perhaps it's stuck. I'll try again."

The door had been stuck, but not badly; for on her first strong push, it groaned inward. She paused on the threshold, suddenly wary; although she could not imagine why. Baffled sunlight smote the drawn curtains; the diffused, uncertain light revealed the outlines of a large four poster bed and the glimmer of an oblong mirror over the dark hulk of a bureau. "Just a bedroom," Jennifer murmured, and overcoming her reluctance, stepped into the room. She threaded her way to the shaded windows and drew the curtains. A shaft of strong sunlight suddenly struck her through the grimy windows, blinding her for an instant.

Turning from the window she blinked, then froze in cold shock. There was a woman lying on the bed. Fully dressed in black, she rested on top of the covers, rigidly staring at the ceiling.

Jennifer dug her nails into the palms of her

hands. She was *not* going to scream again. Slowly, very slowly, breathing from the top of her lungs, she crossed to the bed and stood looking down at the woman.

Aunt Hester.

It was an older Hester than Jennifer remembered, with deep grooves on either side of her painted mouth and puffy pouches under the eyes. The hair was a frizzy orange, instead of the deep brown it once was. But the rouged cheeks and green eyelids, the black chiffon and the golden bracelets on her arms were the same.

Suddenly she felt ill, sick with disgust and anger. Had it been a distorted, overweening ego which had prompted Hester to preserve herself like her husband? Why couldn't the Kirkwoods have died and allowed themselves to be buried decently like everyone else?

Jennifer marched out of the room to the head of the stairs. "Miss Collingwood!" her voice rang out. "Miss Collingwood!"

A few moments later the housekeeper appeared at the bottom of the staircase. "Would you please come up?" Jennifer asked.

"I...I...the stairs...I..."

"Please."

Slowly Miss Collingwood mounted the staircase.

"Come in here a minute," Jennifer said, going to the open door of Hester's bedroom.

The housekeeper reluctantly obeyed; she stood poised just beside the opened door as if ready for flight.

"You knew," Jennifer accused. "You knew all along. Why didn't you tell me?"

"I...I did. When you asked...I said they

64

weren't buried."

Apparently in Miss Collingwood's mind that should have explained everything.

"Mrs. Kirkwood asked you to have this done?"

"Mr. Peters—the taxidermist. She asked him. He did Hubert too."

"She must have been..." *crazy*, Jennifer wanted to say. "She must have been out of her mind."

Was this some kind of grim joke that the old woman had wanted to play on whoever inherited the house? "Here I am," Aunt Hester seemed to say, "in my house, in my bed, and what are you going to do about it?"

"This is bizarre!" Jennifer said, looking down at the implacable face of her dead great-aunt. "What will I do with her, and Hubert?" she cried. "How can I sell the house? I can't show the house to people with...with her here, and Hubert in the library. If people ever knew of this, it would drive them away."

"Maybe," said Miss Collingwood, casting a nervous glance at the immobile Mrs. Kirkwood, "maybe that's exactly what she wanted."

The two women stared at each other in silence.

Suddenly the harsh peal of the doorbell ruptured the quiet. Jennifer started, "who could that be?"

Miss Collingwood raised her brows in answer.

"Not John—oh, Lordy!" Jennifer exclaimed. "I bet it's someone to look at the house. John said he'd tell people it was for sale."

The door bell rang again, insistently, as if the finger on the button were impatient.

"Don't say anything," Jennifer cautioned, forgetting momentarily that "saying anything" was not Miss Collingwood's weakness. "I'll just skip this room and the library."

She followed Miss Collingwood down the stairs. The bell was still ringing. "I'll get it," she told the housekeeper, and then to the door, "Coming! Coming!"

A tall man stood on the doorstep with his back to the sun; so that all Jennifer could make out was straw colored hair and a pair of broad shoulders.

For a few moments neither of them spoke. Then the man asked, "Who are you?"

Taken aback, Jennifer could only stare up at him. "I'm Jennifer Sargent," she said after a moment, shading her eyes against the sun. "Did John McGraw send you?"

"I don't think I know a John McGraw. Should I?" There was a cocky self-assurance to his voice which Jennifer, still smarting from her experience upstairs, found slightly annoying.

"John McGraw, the realtor. The house is up for sale," she explained.

"Oh," he said. "Well, no, I'm not here to buy it. Is old lady Kirkwood selling the place?"

"Mrs. Kirkwood," she said with cold dignity, "died seven months ago."

"And you...you are...?"

"I am her grand-niece. What is your business, please?"

"Aren't you going to ask me in?" he countered, with a flash of very white teeth.

"No," she said. "What is it you want?"

"It's a long story." He shifted his weight and leaned casually against the door jamb, his hands in his pockets. "If I could come in..."

"I don't know you."

"My name is Alex. Alex Kirkwood."

The name stunned her. "He's lying," she told

herself. "He's a quick witted salesman or a con artist, and he's made up the name on the spur of the moment." Jennifer stood obstinately in the door.

"Cross my heart and hope to die," he said, apparently reading the doubt in her eyes. "Hubert Kirkwood was my grandfather."

She suddenly remembered Mr. Emmett's thin, tremulous voice, "Imposters. All of them imposters." And here was one on her doorstep!

"My great-aunt never had any children," she said dryly. "Now if you will excuse me..." She started to close the door, but he put out a large hand and caught it.

"Hubert Kirkwood was my grandfather," he said. "My grandmother was his first wife."

How quick he was, how nimble, how smooth; it was as if he had rehearsed the answers to all the possible questions he might have been asked?

"Can you prove it?" she asked.

"I'm alive, isn't that proof enough?" Again he flashed the white, even-toothed grin.

"That's not what I mean. I had to prove my relationship to the Kirkwoods with a birth certificate, my mother's marriage license, that sort of thing."

"Oh... Well, I suppose I could dig something up."

She had to admit that he had a pleasant voice, but it didn't make up for his brashness. "Why don't you do that and come back later?" She started to close the door again, and, as before, found his hand in the way.

"There's something I'd like to discuss with whoever is in charge," he said.

"I'm in charge. What is it?"

"It's a long story and standing here—well, I feel like a door-to-door salesman."

Jennifer thought that he certainly acted like one and was ready to accuse him; but instead, against her better judgment, she capitulated. "All right. Come in."

He entered the hall, and for a moment Jennifer debated whether to ask him into the parlor or the library. She wondered how he would react to Uncle Hubert, and she was briefly tempted to let him come face to face with the mummified body to see if his maddening, jaunty self assurance could be jolted. But she decided against it. She much preferred getting rid of him as quickly as possible.

"In here," she said, opening the double doors of the parlor.

He moved, she noticed, with a great deal of grace for a big man; and when he sank into a deep chair, she got her first good look at his face.

He was impossibly handsome. No man, outside of a made-up movie actor on the screen, had a right to be that handsome. It was not that his features, taken one by one, were very special. It was the way they were put together; the strong jaw, the definitive nose, the thin, well shaped lips, all combined to make a striking appearance. And there was the contrast of his bright, blond hair and deep, very blue eyes with a beautiful bronze tan that added to his looks.

"You're staring," he said, wagging a finger at her.

"Sorry," she blushed. "You were going to tell me your story." She considered that Hubert had very blue eyes. There was a resemblance. "Silly," she rebuked herself.

"Yes. Hester Kirkwood owes me five thousand dollars. About a year ago she hired me to write her husband's memoirs...."

"And you did?" Jennifer pondered that millions of people had very blue eyes and none of them were related to Hubert Kirkwood.

"I did. The old man, surprisingly, had led an interesting life before he met up with Hester and settled down here. He built this house for her, you know."

"No, I didn't. I thought...well, it looks very old."

"They both liked old houses, the style, I mean. Victorian and all that kind of stuff. It seems well built...."

"It's ugly," Jennifer interposed, feeling a need not to agree with him, not to be pleasant. She wondered if he was telling the truth and was an heir to this house along with her. The whole thing was getting more and more complicated.

"She wouldn't give me all the information I needed," Alex was saying. "Refused to let me mention his first marriage..."

"Didn't she know about it?"

"She did. And she knew about me too, knew that I was a freelance writer. That's why she sent for me. Thought because Hubert was my grandfather, I'd do the book for nothing. We haggled quite a while over the price. Sharp old gal," he shook his head and smiled, "wanted me to gloss over a few of the dirty, underhanded deals Hubert pulled in the business world. He made patent medicines, you know, three quarters water, a good dash of alcohol, artificial flavoring; cherry, strawberry, or orange, depending on what ailed you. He was a bit of a philanderer too. But she wanted a whitewash. So I gave it to her. It's in the car." He waved his hand.

"It's a pity you couldn't have tried to contact her earlier."

"I've been away. On assignment in Alaska...."

"You have?" her voice leapt at him. "Is that where you got your nice tan?"

He grinned at her. "Sun lamp. You'd be surprised how easy and quick it is to get an all over tan with a sun lamp."

"I must try it," she said, acidly. "Anyway, it's too bad about the book. All that work for nothing."

"For nothing? Uh uh." He grinned. "I've got a contract which says five thousand dollars, and five thousand I get out of the estate."

Her heart constricted. "I'll have to consult my lawyer."

He crossed his legs casually and looked around. "Did she leave the whole kit and caboodle to you?" he asked. "Specifically?"

"Yes," she lied as he simultaneously chimed in, "No."

He laughed, and she had to smile, though grudgingly.

"At least half the estate is mine, then," Alex said. "You don't think that's unfair, do you?"

"There's only the house and a small bequest to Miss Collingwood."

"Only the house? I could have sworn the old gal..."

"I wish you wouldn't keep calling her 'old gal,'" Jennifer said irritably.

"Sorry—grandmother. I thought grandmother was loaded; although she was always pretending to be one step from the poorhouse."

"My lawyer would have known if she had had any money, I'm sure."

"Maybe he didn't know. Maybe she stashed it away in old magazines or inside the heads of all these fake statues." His eyes traveled the room speculatively.

Blue eyes or not, she thought he was an imposter and was watching him covertly. He'd memorized a few names, a few facts, got himself through the door and was now sizing up the furniture, the bric-a-brac, the lamps and paintings. What's more, she had a feeling he was lying about the book too. Well, she could find about that right away.

She got to her feet. "Excuse me a moment," she said.

She hurried back to the kitchen. "Miss Collingwood?" The room was empty. Jennifer stood there for a few moments, uncertain, somewhat at a loss. She was so accustomed to Miss Collingwood's presence in the kitchen, she had come to look upon her as a fixture there.

Thinking the housekeeper might be in her room, she went out and turned down the dark passageway. She knocked on the door she remembered—or thought she remembered—as the housekeeper's when from behind her Miss Collingwood said softly, "Miss Sargent?" Jennifer's pulse jumped; The woman had moved so quietly. "Were you looking for me?" The tone was polite, but Jennifer thought she detected a glint of hostility in the housekeeper's dark eyes. Had she been listening outside the parlor?

"Yes," Jennifer said. "I wanted to ask you something. There is a man here . . ." She explained

71

about Alex, his claim that he was Hubert's grandson, that he had been commissioned to write Hubert's memoirs...

"A blond man?" Miss Collingwood asked when she had finished.

Jennifer nodded in the affirmative.

"He's been here before. Yes, he and Mrs. Kirkwood have been writing something. But she never said he was related to her husband. Never."

"Would she have told you if he had been?"

Miss Collingwood thought a moment. "I think so."

"What name did he go by?"

"Why, he was introduced to me as Mr. Donaldson."

"Aha!" Jennifer said. She had him, now. He was a fake, a phony. "How long was he here?" Jennifer asked.

"I don't know. I don't remember how long. I... he left the morning of the day Mrs. Kirkwood took ill."

"Took ill? Was that her last illness?"

"Yes, she died later, some time during that night." Her voice had faded to a hoarse whisper.

"Did this Mr. Donaldson know that Aunt Hester had died?"

"I never saw him again. When he said good-bye, he told me, he was going to Alaska."

So the Alaska part was true. He had sprinkled fiction with fact to make a case for himself. "Thank you, Miss Collingwood."

Jennifer returned to the parlor determined to ease him out of the house. If he had any claims, he could see Mr. Emmett just as she had.

Alex was sitting in the chair where she had left

72

him. But now there was a large bulging, rather shabby piece of brown luggage at his feet. "What's that?" she asked sharply, pointing at it.

"My bag," he said, dimpling at her.

"You aren't staying? she said incredulously.

"Indeed, I am."

"You can't!" She was outraged. "This is my house."

"Correction," he said easily. "*Our* house. And if it bothers you, we'll divide it down the middle. I'll stay in my half." He got to his feet and picked up the bag.

"You have no legal right to remain on the premises." She had to keep herself from shouting. "Besides your name isn't even Kirkwood. You lied. It's Donaldson and..."

"I have as much claim as you do," he said amiably. "And as for my name—which Miss Collingwood supplied you with, no doubt—do you think Hester would have introduced me as a Kirkwood if she wanted the whole world to believe she was the one and only love in Hubert's life?"

He had an answer for everything. She found herself boiling with white anger, "You *can't* stay!"

He looked at her, his eyes widening for a moment. "I promise not to lay a finger on you, and...

She sputtered, unable to find words.

"...and I won't even talk to you, if that's the way you feel. Besides, there's Miss Collingwood. I always imagined she'd make a fine chaperone for some nice, proper prude." And with that he turned his back and walked, with a maddening casualness, out of the room.

CHAPTER VI

Jennifer resisted the urge to pick up a bookend and fling it at Alex's retreating back. His cool audacity and his pure, unmitigated nerve were outrageous. He had bluffed his way into the house, smiled through a dozen pointed questions, and then, unruffled, ignoring her protests, had cooly claimed half of Seacliff Pines and announced his decision to stay.

What was she going to do? Call the sheriff or the police or whoever represented the law in Torrey? Or should she ask John McGraw to throw him out bodily? No, not that. There would be an ugly brawl. She hated fuss, especially violent fuss, and this man who called himself Alex Kirkwood, with his broad shoulders and large hands, did not look like the type who would leave without putting up a bloody battle. Her best bet was to call Mr. Emmett for advice.

She made a hurried shopping list—putting fuses at the top—and left the house. In the garage, to her further chagrin, she found that Alex had installed his car, a fire-engine red sport's model, next to her ancient Pontiac. "Moved in," she thought, "bag and baggage. Well, it won't be for long," she consoled herself.

The general store and post office at Torrey were both housed in one long, single story, gray timbered building. There were several cars parked at a railing to the side of it when Jennifer drove up. One car was being serviced at a gas pump in front of the footworn porch. Inside a dozen people were milling about the aisles that were crowded with cartons, crates and tables which displayed tourist knick-knacks: stamped ash trays, garish satin pillows, cheaply glazed china figurines, and Swiss cuckoo clocks made in Hong Kong.

She found the telephone on the wall beside the ice machine. She hated to discuss her personal affairs in a public place, but there was no choice. The first call she made was to the phone company. Against a background of shuffling feet and dissonant voices, she explained her need for a private phone to a disembodied, bored female who told her she would receive service when "equipment had caught up with demand."

"How soon will that be?" Jennifer wanted to know.

"There's a waiting list," she was told. "It might take two or three months. If you wish, I can take your name..."

"No, thank you," Jennifer said. In two or three months she hoped to be gone.

Next she placed a person to person call to Mr. Emmett. She was informed that he was out of the office and would return in twenty minutes. She decided to have the operator try then.

She strolled over to a nearby counter, within earshot of the phone, and there she stood, to take up time, pretending to be interested in an assortment of painted abalone shells and carved monkey pods. Glancing at the large white-faced Coca Cola clock above the ice machine, she saw that ten minutes had gone by, and then the phone rang. She jumped to answer it and a few seconds later was speaking to Mr. Emmett.

"Oh...is that you?" Mr. Emmett's voice reached her faintly across the miles. "I'm glad you called..."

"Mr. Emmett, there are several things I wanted to talk to you about," she broke in hurriedly, conscious of time and the hands of the Coca Cola clock jerking away second by second, and what each second was costing her. "A man who claims to be Hubert Kirkwood's grandson came to Seacliff Pines this afternoon. He says his name is Alex Kirkwood..."

"Yes, yes. I was just writing you a letter about it. He called yesterday."

"Yesterday?" Then he had known Hester was dead, had known about Mr. Emmett and, probably, about her too. Feeling that Alex had made a bigger fool of her than she had originally thought, her dislike of him widened to a new dimension.

"In the morning, yesterday morning," Mr. Emmett was saying.

"Is he a fake?" she asked sharply, cutting to the heart of the matter.

"I don't really know at this point. You see..."

"You don't *know*?"

"What...? His voice came faintly to her.

"I thought Mr. Kirkwood, Hubert Kirkwood, had been your client for years." She enunciated each word slowly and so loudly that even her own ears rang, "and that you knew all about him."

Mr. Emmett laughed, choking on a cough. A few precious, wheezing seconds passed before he collected himself. "My dear, ahem, ahem...there's a good deal I don't know about most of my clients. Mr. Kirkwood was a hell raiser in his youth, that much I was aware of. He just might, mind you I say, 'might,' have had an early marriage before he met Hester. I can't rule it out."

"Does this Alex have any proof...?"

"He's sending several documents. I'll examine them, of course, look into the matter carefully."

"And if he proves to be what he says he is, half of Seacliff Pines belongs to him?"

"I'm afraid so. But it's a big *if*, you know. Like so many others, he may be an imposter. I really don't think you have too much to worry about."

Cheered somewhat by this partial assurance, Jennifer asked, "In the meantime could I go ahead with trying to sell the house?"

A cough crackled in her ear. "I wouldn't do anything just yet. To play it safe, I'd wait a bit."

"How long?" she wanted to ask, but didn't since she was afraid the answer would be a disappointment. "Then what shall I..." Her voice froze. Through a narrow canyon of soft drink crates she saw Alex's tanned, blond profile. He was examining a large, carved nutcracker made in the shape of a nude female. She wondered if he had followed her and was he close enough to hear.

She turned her back and hunching her shoulders, cupped her hand over the mouthpiece. "What shall I do about this Alex Kirkwood? He's moved himself into the house."

"What's that? My, this is a poor connection. You'll have to speak up, my dear."

She repeated herself, raising her voice, thinking, why should she care if Alex hears her or not?

"Move in, you say? Talk to him. If he is a

gentleman, I am sure he will find other accommodations until this is worked out."

"But this man insists...." Jennifer began.

A nasal twanged voice cut in, "Your three minutes are up."

"Just a minute," Jennifer pleaded. "Don't go away, Mr. Emmett. Mr. Emmett?" She hurriedly fished through her purse, brought out a handful of change and inserted two quarters and a dime, then another quarter. The black box received the coins with a deafening clang. "Mr. Emmett? Mr. Emmett? Are you there?"

"Yes, yes..."

"There's something else. Did you know that Mr. and Mrs. Kirkwood had their bodies preserved by a taxidermist?"

The empty silence which followed indicated that Mr. Emmett did not know.

"They are both in the house," Jennifer went on. "What am I to do with them?"

"My, my," he clucked. "Very unusual, I must say. There's been no provision...let me think. Well, well. I'll have to give that some thought. Since you can't sell the house right away, it's best to leave everything in it as is..."

"But..."

"If the...uh...uh...bodies disturb you, you might tuck them away in a closet or something of that sort."

For some inexplicable reason the thought of the Kirkwood's staring, glassy-eyed behind the closed door of a dark closet seemed more macabre to Jennifer than having them out in the open.

"Ah yes..." She heard Mr. Emmett's faint voice speaking to someone and then, "You'll have to excuse me, Miss Sargent. I have something urgent on the other line. Call me again in a week."

Jennifer hung up feeling vaguely cheated. She wasn't any closer to solving her problems than she had been before she had made her call.

Sidling through the narrow lane of soft drink cases, she peeked around the corner to see if Alex was still in the store. She wanted as little to do with him as possible, to avoid him entirely, if she could. Her eyes noted a corpulent blonde woman in tight green slacks, arguing with a small, barefoot boy who had several candy bars clutched in his hands and a couple examining one of the cuckoo clocks. But no Alex.

Stepping out from her hiding place, she received a tap on her shoulder. Her head swung around, and Alex grinned at her. "Looking for someone?"

She faced him, conscious of an embarrassed flush staining her cheeks. "Yes, you," she said annoyed with him and with herself. "I've just talked to my lawyer."

"Mr. Emmett?"

"Yes, Mr. Emmett. You lied to me, you know. You knew Hester Kirkwood had died."

"Lied? You never asked me whether I knew she had died, and I never said she hadn't. As I remember it, my one comment on the subject was, 'Is old lady Kirkwood selling the place?' "

"But the implication was..."

"Your own interpretation."

She glared at him for a moment. "My lawyer..."

"*Ours*," he corrected mildly, leaning against the crates, watching her with an amused smile.

"Mr. Emmett, *my* lawyer, said that if you were any kind of decent gentleman..."

79

"Has anyone told you that you are very pretty when you get mad? Brown eyes snapping and..."

"*Mr. Emmett*," she interrupted, literally gritting her teeth, "feels that under the circumstances, a *gentleman* would find other accommodations until his claim was verified."

"A gentleman." He shook his head. "Sorry to disappoint you, Jenny..."

"It's *Jennifer*!"

"... but I'm not a gentleman. Aside from that, I won't leave, one—because I have fallen madly in love with you..."

"Please, spare me the..."

"... two, I'm crazy about the house, which is half mine and, three, I want my five thousand dollars."

Jennifer stared at him, a tiny pulse beating in her throat. "Well," she said, "you can whistle for it."

Alex's smile vanished, and his eyes turned a deep, dark blue. For an awful moment Jennifer wondered if he was going to hit her. But the grin suddenly returned. "That's another thing I like about you; you speak your mind."

Jennifer fumed all the way back to Seacliff Pines. She couldn't remember a time when she had so turned against a man—anyone. Mr. Goodbody, in his worst moments, had never aroused such frustrated anger in her. She had only known Alex for a few brief hours, but she did not think their relationship had the slightest chance of improving with time. His whole manner went against the grain.

Was part of it, she asked herself, because she was afraid he really might turn out to be Hubert Kirkwood's grandson, and she would have to share her inheritance? She hated to think that Aunt Hester's will had turned her into a venal, hard headed shrew, fighting tooth and nail over an ugly Victorian house.

No, it wasn't the house or the money it represented. She disliked Alex because he was so self-assured, so certain he could have his way simply by using the currency of his golden smile. Soft spoken, confident, the kind of man women found irrestible, he was also the kind of man who took full advantage of his nervy charm. Men like that turned her stomach.

If he had been a decent sort—say someone like John McGraw—she might have accepted him after the initial shock; in fact, a trustworthy ally would relieve many of her worries. He'd know what to do with those two—Hubert and Hester— for instance, their bodies in their appalling life-like mummification. An able person would help in cleaning up the place and might make a few necessary repairs. No, she would not mind sharing the house under those circumstances, but not with Alex, even if by some miracle he did turn out to be a rightful heir.

As she drove through the gate, she saw John McGraw's car turn in behind her. She waved her hand out the window, and in her rear view miror, saw him wave back.

"Thank God, for John," she thought, "sane, solid, uncomplicated."

He helped her carry the groceries into the house, then obligingly found the fuse box and installed the new fuses Jennifer had bought.

"That's better," Jennifer said as the lights went on and the refrigerator began to purr.

"The car work okay?" John asked.

"Fine, I called Mr. Emmett when I was at the store." She told him about Alex.

His face darkened as she spoke. "Is that all the lawyer could do for you? Tell you to wait."

"Seems he has to, quote, 'look into the matter.' And...Oh! How could I have forgotten? Hester Kirkwood's upstairs."

"What?"

"She's stuffed like Hubert."

"My God."

"You can say that again. Two corpses and Alex Kirkwood." She reached into a bag and brought out several apples, giving one to John.

"Why didn't this man come forward sooner and make his claim?" John asked.

"He says he was in Alaska."

"I bet."

"It's impossible to trip him up. I've tried."

"He sounds like a pain."

"He is." Jennifer bit into her apple, chewing slowly. "It's hard for me to understand why Mr. Emmett doesn't know more about the Kirkwoods."

"He's probably not getting much of a fee, so there's no incentive to know more than the bare essentials. Mr. Emmett thought it would be a simple case."

She sighed. "So did I."

He put an arm around her shoulders. "Buck up, it can't be all that bad. If you like, I'll talk to the sheriff and see if we can't get this Alex what's-his-name thrown out.

"No," she said. "I...if it turns out he's right..."

"One chance in a million."

"All right, one chance in a million, but it would

be terribly embarrassing if he *was* Alex Kirkwood."

"Put ground glass in his coffee and sand in the sugar bowl."

She laughed, "Stay for dinner? No ground glass, I promise."

"Okay, if you insist." He leaned over and kissed her cheek just as Alex poked his head in the door.

"Say, Jenny, where do you keep the towels?" he asked in an off-hand, but offensively familiar voice.

"Ask Miss Collingwood," she said, reddening with anger. She wondered how long he had been listening at the door.

When he had gone, John said, "Do you want me to bust his nose?"

"No," she sighed. "What good would it do?"

It was long past midnight when Jennifer awoke suddenly from a confused nightmare to the rasping shrillness of the doorbell. Her first thought was that the bell had been part of her dream; but a moment later the sound came again, shrieking up the stairs with its hoarse, blatant summons.

Thinking that there was no point in waiting for Miss Collingwood to answer it, she leaped out of bed. The housekeeper probably never stirred from under her covers until the light of day. She drew on her robe and stuffing her feet hurriedly into slippers, went out. Switching on the light at the top of the stairs, she ran down, slid the bolt back and cracked the door open. "Who is it?" she asked of a bulky shadow.

"Miss Leila Dee," a loud contralto voice echoed in the dark night. "Are you the housekeeper?"

"No," said Jennifer. She hoped it wasn't someone to look at the house at this time of night.

"Then you must be the niece."

"Yes," said Jennifer, "I'm..."

"Miss Sargent? Am I speaking to Miss Sargent?"

"Yes."

"Aren't you going to let me in?" It was a commanding voice, the kind one didn't argue with.

"Just a minute." Jennifer undid the chain and opened the door. Brushing past her, the owner of the imperious voice came into the hall. She was a short, stout woman with a double-chinned face no longer youthful but trying valiantly to appear so. Bright spots of carmine highlighted each wrinkled-webbed cheek; heavy lipstick delineated the mouth; and false, beaded eyelashes fluttered beneath penciled brows. In the overhead light her face looked like that of an aging, painted clown.

"You certainly took your time," the woman said. "It's cold out there." She wore a mangy fur stole, swathed in defiance across a preening pigeon's chest, and a green skirt, stopping at a point above the knees of a surprisingly good pair of legs.

"Who's that? Jennifer said noticing another shadow of a figure.

"It's Charlie," the woman said over her shoulder.

A wizened-faced man with an unlit cigar stuck in one corner of his mouth, a short man, not much taller than the woman, came struggling through the door, a suitcase in each hand.

"My chauffeur," the woman said airily to an

84

astonished Jennifer. "You might give him a hand."

Jennifer gaped at her for a moment, then dutifully lugged in the last of the suitcases; five in all, they were cheap, powder blue suitcases.

"Who was she? Where did she come from?" a bewildered Jennifer asked herself silently.

"Ah, thank you." The woman put out a gloved hand, and Jennifer limply shook it. "I'm Leila Dee, Hester Kirkwood's life long friend."

Jennifer's mind searched for the right question among the many thronging her brain.

"*The* Miss Leila Dee," the stout woman preened.

Should she know her? Jennifer probed back into her memory and drew a blank. "I'm sorry. I don't..."

Miss Dee waved aside Jennifer's stumbling uncertainty. "I was in burlesque, a star, a headliner, from coast to coast. Fans and bubbles were my specialty. But then," her eyes creased as she examined Jennifer, "that was before your time. You're just a child and wouldn't have heard. Fame dies, you know."

"Yes," said Jennifer. She wondered how Leila Dee knew her name, knew that she was at Seacliff Pines. "Had you heard about my great-aunt? She died some seven months ago."

"Ah yes, and I cried. How I cried! Didn't I, Charlie?"

Charlie made some incoherent comment, shifting the cigar in his mouth.

"Hester and I were in burlesque together, you know," said Leila Dee, wiping an imaginary tear from the corner of her eye.

"I didn't know," Jennifer said. "I always understood my aunt was on the stage."

"It was the stage, my dear. Burlesque *is* stage. I know Hester, after she married, liked to put it down. But it's a grand profession. And anyway Hester never made it out of the chorus." She removed her gloves from fingers that sparkled with rings. Looking around, pursing her red lips, she said, "So—this is Seacliff Pines. How sweet of Hester to leave it all to me."

CHAPTER VII

Jennifer wanted to laugh, to shout, to weep. Irrational as she knew it to be, she nevertheless blamed the distant, doddering Mr. Emmett for Miss Leila Dee (and her shadow, Charlie) and this latest complication. How many more heir apparents would find their way to the door?

"I beg your pardon," Jennifer said, recovering somewhat, and hoping rather desperately that her ears had deceived her.

"Hester always said she wanted me to have Seacliff Pines," Leila Dee said, going to the staircase and running a finger over the carved newel post. She rapped on it smartly. "Good solid wood. Where's the parlor?"

"In there," Jennifer said, motioning with her head. "But I..."

Leila Dee tottered across the carpet on platform soles and opened the parlor doors. Her hand found a switch, and the lamps scattered throughout the room suddenly sprang to life, their various shades throwing pebbled shadows against the wall. "Lovely!" Miss Dee exclaimed.

"I *am* sorry," said Jennifer, trailing behind her. "My aunt made no mention of you in her will."

"I know that," said Leila Dee, picking up a japanned cigarette box. "She didn't mention you, either." She turned, her mascara-lined eyes narrowing. "Isn't that right?"

"N...not exactly." The woman was well informed. Had she wheedled her information from Mr. Emmett?

"Real Tiffany," Miss Dee said, fingering a lamp. "Not one of those Sears Roebuck fakes."

"I spoke to my lawyer today," Jennifer said, "and he did not tell me about you."

"Mr. Emmett. Yes, indeed. We had a long talk this evening by phone. He's a little deaf. But I think he got the message." She turned her head and called, "Charlie? Come on in, Charlie, and see what we've got here."

Charlie crossed the threshold. He peered around sourly, then seated himself on a tapestry covered chair, leaning back and tapping his fingers on the gilt arms.

"What do you think?" Leila Dee asked him.

"Could do with some fixin' up," he said. "Looks like a damned museum."

"Treasures, Charlie," she admonished. "Treasures! But we'll fix it up too." She went to the mantel and stood looking up at Hester's portrait. "A dear friend, a dear friend," she sighed heavily.

"Miss Dee..." Jennifer began. "I don't like to seem—well, impolite. But I don't know you and..."

"Oh, dear child, I understand. I have a letter here..." She snapped open a pouched handbag and withdrew a folded sheet of paper. "This is a copy. The original went to Mr. Emmett. But I think after you've read it, you'll be able to tell what's what." She pushed the paper into Jennifer's hand. "Go ahead," she invited, "read it."

The letter dated April 9, 1974, was written in a stilted hand. There was some mention of Hester and Leila's mutual friendship, a long, rambling description of Seacliff Pines and mention of

Hester's stiff knee and elbow joints. The important part of the letter was in the last paragraph which read: "I love this house so. Hubert had it built especially for me, you know. And when I die, I want you to have it. It's yours as long as you live in it—a home for your old age. It will be small payment for your having introduced me to Hubert, the love of my life. Yours ever, Hester."

Was it a forgery? Jennifer had never received any written communication from Hester; therefore she wasn't acquainted with her handwriting. Mr. Emmett, of course, in his slow, procrastinating way might get around to checking it. But even so, she wondered if a letter was legally acceptable in matters of inheritance.

"The letter," said Leila Dee, taking it from Jennifer, "supersedes the will. The will was made out in March of this year."

"Oh?" said Jennifer. Was she a fake, an imposter? She could have known Hester years ago and on hearing of her death, improvised and forged the letter. "How did you know my aunt died?"

"I read about it in the papers. That ad, you know." She shrugged free of her stole, brushed it lovingly with her hand, then carefully placed it across the seat of a wide upholstered chair.

"The ad hasn't been running for some time," Jennifer said with forced patience. "And..."

"Charlie, here, caught it and showed it to me."

Charlie, who had pushed a low table over and had stretched his legs out on it, grunted. "S'right, I was the one who seen it."

"Get your feet off the furniture, Charlie, dear," Leila Dee scolded.

Charlie obliged with another grunt.

"If Mrs. Kirkwood wanted you to have the house," Jennifer continued to argue, feeling as though history, her history, was repeating itself monotonously, "she would have said so."

"She did," Miss Dee stated matter-of-factly, "in the letter." She seated herself on the sofa and crossed her legs, showing a good deal of plump thigh. From her purse she took an ivory holder and a chipped, enamel cigarette case. "I've always wanted," she said, snapping the case open and choosing a cigarette, "to retire in the country, a nice cozy place by the sea. Ain't that right, Charlie?"

"That's right."

"And this is just perfect," she said.

Jennifer felt the blood draining from her face. "Miss Dee—really, I think before you plan on retiring to Seacliff Pines, you will have to prove you're entitled to it."

"Well," she said, inserting the cigarette in the ivory holder. "I already have."

At least Alex had offered to share the house. "You won't think me dense, if I don't agree," said Jennifer with an icy smile.

"Suit yourself, dearie."

"And I'm not about to move out, simply because you think the house is yours," Jennifer went on. "Mr. Emmett, you know, will have to decide."

"I am sure he'll decide in my favor. But you can stay until he does, if that's what you want," she offered grandly.

Jennifer, momentarily speechless, could only stare at Miss Leila Dee, the former burlesque queen, who wanted so much to retire in country. She and Alex would make a pair. She could hardly wait to see them lock horns. "Hubert Kirkwood's grandson is here," Jennifer said, hoping that information was news and would jolt Leila Dee out of her complacency.

"Hubert didn't have a grandson," she said, lighting her cigarette. "The man's putting you on."

Jennifer shrugged, "he doesn't think so."

"We'll see," she said.

Jennifer moved to the door. "If you'll excuse me, I'm going back to bed."

"Go ahead, dearie. I'm a night owl. Just tell me where I can find the housekeeper."

"The housekeeper?"

"Yes, Mr. Emmett says there's a housekeeper, Collins, something like that. She's here, isn't she?"

"Miss Collingwood. Yes, but she's sleeping."

"I'd like a bite to eat and then my bed made up. Charlie here drives, but won't do anything else."

Jennifer, tired and worn by interrupted sleep, shock and frustration, decided that Miss Collingwood would simply have to handle the latest uninvited guest to the Pines herself. "Her room is down the hall, past the kitchen, the third or fourth one," Jennifer said. "And now if you'll excuse me."

"Good night, dearie."

"That's a hard customer," Jennifer thought, climbing the stairs, "hard as nails in spite of all the 'dearies.' "

The next morning Jennifer got up early and slipped quietly out of the house. On her way to the garage she saw Leila Dee's car parked in the driveway, an old white Ford covered with the yellow dust of travel. They had come in a hurry, she and Charlie (was he really her chauffeur?), in the middle of the night. Leila Dee was obviously

91

afraid that she might be too late. The ad calling for the heirs of the Kirkwood estate had long since ceased to run, as Jennifer had pointed out; so Leila—or Charlie—must have discovered it in an old newspaper. She pictured Charlie unwrapping some coffee mugs, or cheap glasses recently purchased at the variety store, and running his tobacco stained finger down the ads, exclaiming, "Didn't you used to know a Hester Kirkwood?" She could just see Leila Dee grasping the paper. "Here let me see that. Why—sure. Hester. She's the one who married Hubert Kirkwood." Leila must have pondered and thought for a while and then sat down to draw up the first draft of the letter.

"Well," Jennifer thought as she maneuvered the Pontiac out of the garage and past the Ford, "I'll soon know."

She drove into Torrey where she had to wait a half hour before the sleepy eyed storekeeper unlocked the door. A tall, thin man with a mole on his left cheek, who had never personally waited on her, looked at her now so questioningly that she felt she ought to introduce herself. He in turn told her that his name was Schofield, but everybody called him Dutch.

"Seacliff Pines?" he said, after Jennifer had explained that Hester Kirkwood had been her great-aunt and that she was staying there until the estate was settled. "You know, I've lived in these parts for twenty years and never seen it. The Kirkwoods weren't customers," he added. "Didn't even know that Mrs. Kirkwood died until a month ago. Must have had the funeral in San Francisco."

"Yes," Jennifer lied, surmising that Dutch acted

as the local gossip, and the truth would shock the whole town.

"Did she leave you the house?" Dutch asked, plucking a toothpick from a cup near the cash register.

"The estate hasn't been settled," Jennifer answered, wondering how she could ease herself out of the conversation.

"Had a pile of money, I hear." He began to pick at his teeth.

"I wouldn't know," said Jennifer, drawing her mouth into a smile. "Do you mind if I use the phone?"

"Be my guest. It's public. Need change?"

"No, thanks. I think I can manage."

She made her way to the phone, conscious of Dutch being all ears and leaning forward on the counter behind her. She fumbled with her coins, counting and recounting them, stalling for time until a minute later a customer arrived and distracted the storekeeper's attention. It was then she put in her call.

The connection was poor, and Mr. Emmett, never keen eared, had her repeat everything two and sometimes three times. The gist of their hazardous exchange was that Mr. Emmett felt there might be some validity to Miss Dee's claim. "I'll have an expert check the writing," he said. "The problem, you understand, is that the will is so vague."

"Did you draw it up?" she couldn't help asking.

"What? No, my dear," he said, rather hurt. "I'm a *good* lawyer. The will was drawn up by Hester Kirkwood herself. She wanted it that way. I'm so sorry, Miss Sargent. Why don't you call back in, say, a week or two. Perhaps I can give you something more definite then."

A week or two. And what was she to do in the meantime? Wait. She saw before her the hours, the days, the nights stretching endlessly; her patience tested at each unpleasant encounter with Alex and Leila Dee—and Miss Collingwood. But she did not dream of giving up, not then. She planned to go right ahead and do her cleaning and to pretend they weren't there. Both Alex and Miss Dee were fakes—she was as sure of that as she was of the sun coming up in the east and going down in the west, and she was not going to let them drive her from her original plan.

Her resolve was strengthened when she got back to the house and found Alex tinkering with his sport's car in the garage. He had taken over all the available space, spreading himself out, tools, rags, motor parts scattered across the concrete floor.

"Sorry," Alex said, coming up to her as she waited, motor running. "I'll get this stuff out of your way, pronto." Then leaning on her window. "Out early, aren't you?"

She gave him a cold look. "Right."

"I understand we have guests."

"Have you met them?"

"No. Still sleeping. I heard them come in last night, and Miss Collingwood told me who they were. Competition, eh?"

"Not for me," she said.

He started to reply, then shrugged and went back inside. He shoved the jumbled mess into a corner, and Jennifer drove the car in. She got out of the car and without looking at him, with lips pressed firmly together, went into the house.

Miss Collingwood called to her as she was climbing the stairs. "Miss Sargent, may I have a word with you?"

"Yes...?" she said, coming down to the first step.

"There was a woman who came to my door last night..."

"Oh, yes. She arrived late. I let her in. Said she was a friend of Aunt Hester's, Leila Dee. You don't know her?"

Miss Collingwood's look was blank.

"She's never been here before?"

"No."

"Do you recall Mrs. Kirkwood ever speaking of her?"

"Never. This... this woman, she says the house is hers."

Jennifer lowered her voice. "She thinks, she has a claim, but I rather doubt it. Mr. Emmett is making an investigation."

"She asked me to stay on as her housekeeper."

Jennifer swallowed her irritation. "She is ahead of herself, Miss Collingwood." So Leila Dee was going to make an ally of the frightened, little housekeeper. "And did you agree?"

"I told her I couldn't make the stairs, but she said that was all right, as long as I fixed her meals. She said that she'd start paying me now. But you don't think she owns the house?"

"Frankly no."

"Well, I..." Miss Collingwood's face suddenly

whitened. There was a heart beat's pause, and then she grasped Jennifer's wrist. "Do you hear that?"she whispered fiercely.

Jennifer, caught off guard, felt a wave of cold terror sweep over her, raising the hairs on her arms and back of her neck.

"Now ... Miss Collingwood ..."

"Shhh!"

To Jennifer's ears, sharpened by fright, came the sound of a brassy tinkle, the same jingle-jangle she had heard her first night at Seacliff Pines. "It's a beaded lamp caught in a draft," she heard her voice say, while her mind said, "Bracelets! Aunt Hester's bracelets."

Jennifer's head turned slowly, her eyes staring up into the gloom. A board creaked. The clock in the corner ticked heavily, beating time with Jennifer's heart. She knew the greater part of her fright was nonsense, that rationally Aunt Hester, what was left of her, was stuffed with cotton batting, and that the house, even in daylight, lent itself readily to suggestion. One could whisper "spook" or "ghost" and, like a chameleon changing color, the dark shadows seemed to slowly spread like inkstains blotting out light, transforming shape and perspective. But it was hard to think rationally with one's brain frozen in fear, waiting for the unknown, the unexpected. In a matter of seconds it came, a sudden hollow thud followed by a high pitched screech, sending Jennifer's heart jarring against her ribs.

A moment later a cat, a gray cat, came tearing down the stairs. It ran past the two women to the door and began clawing at the glass.

"Lordy...!" Jennifer let out her breath and

gently untangled herself from Miss Collingwood's frightened grasp. "It's just a cat." She opened the door, and the cat flew out onto the veranda and down the stairs.

"It shouldn't be in the house," Miss Collingwood said in a shaky voice.

"Does it belong here?"

"No," said Miss Collingwood, but I recognize it. It's a stray from somewhere. Mrs. Kirkwood hated cats."

"I wonder how it got in...." Jennifer mused.

"Do you think you might take it with you, next time you go out in the car, and lose it?"

Jennifer stared at the housekeeper. "*Lose* it?"

"Maybe it would be better to drown it."

"I couldn't do that," Jennifer said, somewhat shocked. "Do you hate cats, too?"

"Yes," said Miss Collingwood after a moment. "They scare me." She blinked her eyes. "Am I supposed to cook for that man too?"

"Which man?" Jennifer asked, confused by the sudden switch from cats to men.

"Mr. Alex."

"Not unless he offers to pay you as Miss Dee did."

"I'm only getting one hundred and fifty dollars a month from the lawyer," she said in a thin voice.

"Is that all?" Jennifer had been told the bequest was small, but she hadn't realized how meagre a sum it was.

"That's all," said Miss Collingwood, her eyes wide and moist. "I...I worked very hard. Thirty years." She turned her head away, her underlip trembling.

Jennifer, instantly sympathetic, took her hand.

"Perhaps that was all Mrs. Kirkwood could give you."

The housekeeper snatched her hand away, her face contorting weirdly, her eyes flashing with anger. The change was so sudden it startled Jennifer. It was as if the mouse had suddenly turned into a bare-fanged lion.

"She...she hated me," Miss Collingwood said hoarsely in a low, furious voice. "All these years she hated me. She did it—wrote that will out of spite. Mr. Kirkwood was kind to me, and she hated me for it."

"If she felt that way about you, why didn't you leave?" Jennifer asked.

"I..." Anger drained from her as swiftly as it had come. "I...I couldn't." She wrung her hands, shaking her head.

Jennifer waited, thinking Miss Collingwood would say more, but no explanation came.

"You felt the house should be yours?" Jennifer asked.

"No...not the house. I don't care about the house. But one hundred and fifty."

"I didn't get *any* money," Jennifer consoled. "The lawyer said my great-aunt had none."

Miss Collingwood looked at her out of red rimmed eyes. "She was rich," she whispered. "Rich!" Then her eyes suddenly slanted upward, staring at the top of the stairs. Her body turned rigid.

"No," Jennifer told herself, "I'm not going to listen. I'm not going to look."

The housekeeper held this pose for several moments while Jennifer mentally blocked out her hearing and held her breath. Then Miss Collingwood relaxed and said in her normal voice, "I'll get supper. I don't mind cooking for you; since you buy the groceries."

Jennifer had never imagined Miss Collingwood capable of such anger, never dreamed that anything but a close and affectionate relationship had existed between Hester and her housekeeper. Of course, Miss Collingwood's terrible fear of her employer's ghost should have given her a clue, but Jennifer had thought that the housekeeper's firm belief in a supernatural presence at Seacliff Pines—whoever or whatever—was what scared Miss Collingwood. Now she wondered.

"She hated me!" Miss Collingwood had said with venom. Apparently the feeling had been shared. Why? What had made the two women, isolated from the world, disliking each other so intensely, and yet stay together all those years, living in each other's constant presence? Perhaps the two of them had been bound together in mutual dependence; although Jennifer, thinking of Hester's set jaw in the portrait above the parlor mantel, rather doubted her great-aunt had ever been dependent on anyone.

And what part had Hubert played in this little drama? Miss Collingwood, according to her own words, had been at Seacliff when Hubert was still alive. "He was kind to me." Was there a little dalliance between them, a mild affair? Thirty years ago Miss Collingwood must have been more appealing, perhaps not quite so mousy; and Hubert, reputedly, had a roving eye. But if that were the case, if Hester had been suspicious, jealous, had found them out, why hadn't she simply replaced Miss Collingwood with someone old and ugly?

It was one more mystery connected with Hester

Kirkwood and with Seacliff Pines, but one, Jennifer assured herself, that need not concern her. What did it matter? Hadn't she resolved to go about her business without getting involved? She hadn't even finished inspecting the house, let alone cleaning it. She still had no idea how many rooms there were, how many bedrooms, baths, closets or storerooms. When Mr. Emmett gave her the go-ahead signal, she wanted to be ready to sell the house so that she could leave as quickly as possible. She would have to keep her promise to Miss Collingwood about finding a place for her, of course, but that could be done later when everything else was settled.

For now, she thought, she might as well get on with looking the house over. She went upstairs and changed into old jeans and a sweater. The bedroom door had swung open before she could get her shoes on, and when she went to shut it; she heard a sharp click in the corridor. Poking her head out cautiously, she saw Alex quietly, stealthily closing the door of Hester's bedroom.

"Paying your respects?" she asked sarcastically, and was secretly delighted to see him whirl about in surprise.

His recovery, however, was almost instantaneous. "Why didn't anyone tell me...?" He made a wry face.

"I thought I'd let you find out for yourself."

"Weird," he said.

"Yes. You can go in any time you like. And you needn't be furtive about it." She was breaking her earlier resolution by speaking to him. But catching him at an awkward moment and having the upper hand was too good an opportunity to be missed.

"Was I furtive?" he asked, moving toward her.

"Yes," she said. "You looked like a second-story man who'd just heisted the family's jewels."

"How would you know what a second-story man looks like?"

He was standing over her now. She hadn't realized how tall he was, how wide his shoulders; nor had she been aware of the aura he exuded, an aura of masculinity, of danger, and a charm which she sensed could be both persuasive and perilous to her. "I don't know," she said. "Just used my imagination."

"Oh?"

The "oh?" she knew intuitively had many meanings. She wanted to turn away, to end the conversation, but couldn't think how to do so without showing her sudden discomfort. "I thought you were in the garage fixing your car."

"I got bored with it and decided to come up here and have a look around."

"Look around? I should think you'd know the house backward and forward, since you were living in it before Aunt Hester died."

"I wasn't living here," he said. "Old Hester wanted to charge me ten dollars a night for my bed. So I just stayed at the lodge up the road where the company was—well, shall I say, a little more exciting?"

"Why don't you stay there now, then."

"Because *now*, it happens, the excitement is all here."

He smiled down at her, and she felt the blood rising to her face. There was a long silence during which his eyes held hers in a hypnotic gaze, the dark pupils seeming to grow larger and larger until

Jennifer felt they would engulf her. Finally, when she thought she could not bear the tension any longer, she said, "I have things to do," and turned to go back into her room.

He caught her arm. "Couldn't we be friends?" His touch fired the red in her cheeks to flame.

"No," she said in a muffled voice, jerking her arm away.

Afterwards, after she had closed the door on his puzzled face, she sat on the bed for a long time listening to her heart slowly return to its normal beat. She hated herself for losing her poise in front of that man. He was probably chuckling to himself now, recalling how he had made her blush, congratulating himself because one more female had turned all weak and flustered at his smile, his touch.

Jennifer angrily punched her fist into the nubbed bedspread. "Damn him!" she muttered.

She waited a few minutes longer, then tucking her shirt in, went out and started her rounds of the second floor. Her mind, however, was still on Alex, and she thought of all the clever, devastating remarks she might have uttered. Her imaginary debate continued as she drifted from room to room, vaguely conscious of dim, clouded mirrors, high beds, and dusty, thick clawed bureaus. She did not come out of her mental fog until she stumbled into Leila Dee's room. Dressed in a pink, feather trimmed negligee, the former burlesque star was stretched out on a chaise lounge, filing her nails. She looked up sharply as Jennifer came through the door.

"Haven't you got manners?" she asked huffily. "I was always taught to knock."

102

"Sorry," Jennifer apologized.

From then on she knocked on each door before entering. One room was Charlie's (she smelled the cigar smoke), and another, at the end of the hall, was Alex's (she recognized his sweater).

The house was much larger than she had thought. There was still a third story, broken up by cupolas and dormered rooms, and above that was the turret. She decided to by-pass the third story, for the time being, and went directly up to the turret.

The room, she could see at a glance, had been used as a storeroom. She recognized the canned goods, Miss Collingwood had spoken of, arranged in high, neat rows. It was an airless, dim place, the light coming in from three long, narrow windows covered with drawn, weather streaked shades. There was the usual attic medley; broken lamps, an old radio, frayed, cane bottom chairs, rusty umbrellas, cartons and cartons of green glass jars and old bottles.

Jennifer threaded her way across the wooden floor and rolled up one of the shades. On the dusty sill at her feet lay dead, dehydrated flies; and a thin, silvery web had been spun across the lower corner of the glass. Peering through the grimy window, Jennifer could see a wedge of the sea brimming with blue sunlight in the distance. Directly below was the stone terrace. It looked very far away.

Suddenly, behind her, the door wheezed and banged shut. She spun around, instantly alert. Silence hung in the heavy air, a silence so complete that not even the sea could be heard, the sea which insistently, constantly made itself known in every other nook and cranny of Seacliff Pines. The room which she had thought large when she first came through the door, seemed to have grown infinitely smaller, the clutter to have multiplied, the walls to have come nearer. Her recently acquired fear of closed places suddenly rose in a sour lump to her throat.

"Don't panic," she told herself. "Doors closed without apparent reason, all through the house." But it was more than the closing door which held her breathless at the window. It was an intuitive, hair raising sensation. *"There's someone here. Somebody watching me..."*

"No," she pushed the thought away, "no." Was she becoming paranoic too? "There is no one in this room," she repeated silently, wiping her sweaty palms along the sides of her jeans. Still she stood immobolized, her gaze slowly, fearfully traveling past tiered cans, cane bottom chairs, puckered and dented lampshades. But the corners of the room eluded her, hidden by shadow and the shapes of anonymous discards. She looked across the room at the door. Its position, too, seemed to have changed in perspective. She viewed it, her escape hatch, down a long, narrow vista bordered by tall stacks of canned peaches, old brown cartons and dusty, broken tables.

Her mouth dry, she took a step forward.

A sudden stunning blow on the back of her right shoulder sent her reeling, crashing into cans and boxes, knocking them over, scattering them across the floor. She staggered to keep herself upright, and, as a large can bounced off her foot she hardly felt its sharp weight. She stumbled to the door, flung it open and skidded, half-fell, down the stairs.

Even in her hurried, horrified flight, she was aware of the attic door above whining shut as if a hand had reached out to close it.

CHAPTER VIII

Jennifer sat on the bed, staring at the large ugly bruise across the top of her right foot where the can had hit it. She had expected to find a bruise on her shoulder too, but strangely enough there was none. And because there was none, it disturbed her. Had she imagined that blow which had sent her reeling? Had it just been in her mind, a supposition caused by her sudden panic at the closed door and the airless, dim attic? During those awful moments when she had come stumbling down the stairs, it had crossed her mind that perhaps she had been too bullheaded about the non-existence of ghosts. But now that she was safe in her room with sunlight rippling over the carpet, warmly illuminating the heavy furniture and her shoes lined up on the floor of the closet, she dismissed the idea of ghosts as momentary weak mindedness.

Her shoulder did ache, though, especially when she moved it. That proved the blow had been real; didn't it? And if that were so, then somebody had been hiding in the attic; somebody had been there before she had entered it; somebody taken by surprise perhaps and not wanting his or her identity known. The blow must have been meant for her head, but her attacker had been either inept or had miscalculated.

Could it have been Alex? Somehow he did not fit

her picture of an awkward assailant; he walked and moved with the deliberate, easy coordination of an athlete in perfect control. And he was much taller than she. If he had wanted to bash in her skull, he would have done a very thorough job of it.

No, her attacker most likely had been clumsy and short. Miss Collingwood? Except for the time Jennifer had coaxed her up to Hester's room, she had never seen the housekeeper climb the stairs to upper floors. And she seemed so frail. Jennifer could not imagine those thin wrists and the fluttering hands capable of striking even a glancing blow.

Leila Dee was short, stout and assertive. She was the kind of woman who would believe in a direct action like hitting someone in the head.

Or was it Charlie? He looked more bored than evil, but he would obey any order from Leila.

Jennifer, on a sudden impulse, got up and went to Charlie's room. She rapped lightly on the door and when there was no answer, twisted the knob and opened it. Charlie was in bed, lying on his side, snoring in breathy fits and starts. Was he pretending? Jennifer watched him for a few moments and then went across the hall and knocked on Leila's door.

"Who is it?" the contralto voice called.

"Jennifer."

There were scuffling sounds. "Just a minute."

Jennifer patiently waited for much more than a minute and finally Miss Dee, in the same feathered, pink negligee, opened the door.

"Well, dearie, what is it again?" Leila Dee asked irritably.

"May I come in?"

"What for?"

"I want to talk to you for a minute."

"Oh, all right."

Jennifer, feeling uncomfortable because she did not know how to approach the question uppermost in her mind, looked around for a place to sit. The unmade bed was strewn with dresses, slacks, stockings, as were the two chairs. Leila Dee had already taken the chaise lounge and lolling back on the cushions, was fitting a cigarette to her holder. "What is it that's so important?" she asked in a bored voice.

Jennifer gingerly lowered herself onto the edge of the bed. "I spoke to Mr. Emmett this morning," she began, "and he is looking into the matter of your letter."

"Is he?" She drew languidly on her cigarette, made a round "O" of her painted mouth and through it blew a series of smoke rings.

"Yes," said Jennifer. "Have you seen the rest of the house?"

"Not yet."

So she hadn't found Hubert or Hester. But then, Jennifer did not think the two preserved figures would disturb Leila Dee. Somehow, the woman did not seem the kind of person who quailed easily.

"... I'm writing to my decorator, asking him to come down," Leila Dee was saying. "See what he says. I'd like to redo the parlor."

"What about the attic?"

Leila Dee looked over at her with raised, penciled brows. "Well—now. Come to the point. What's bugging you?"

"Someone tried to clobber me."

"In the attic?" She laughed, an uproarious, hearty laugh.

"It isn't funny," Jennifer said.

"Why should I clobber you? When the time comes I'll just get a court order and have you thrown out. No, I haven't been to the attic. I've been resting. I tell you we had a time getting here last night. Charlie got lost three times."

"Charlie...is he...has he been employed by you for long?"

"He's a friend. And if you're thinking *he* hit you, forget it. Charlie doesn't go around hitting women."

She stubbed her cigarette out in a figured cloisonne bowl. "By the way, is that divine looking man the one who calls himself Hubert's grandson?"

"Yes. Have you met him?"

"We said hello when I went down to get a cup of coffee. No resemblance. Not at all. Some gall to think the house is his."

"Half," Jennifer corrected.

"And the housekeeper, the old maid in the kitchen. What does she want?"

"Nothing," said Jennifer.

Leila Dee narrowed her eyes. "I don't believe it. Everyone wants something. Including you. Now...now, no need to get your back up. I've lived a little longer than you, dearie, and I know what makes people tick. I can't blame you. You think you're on to a good thing, pretending to be Hester's great niece. I don't know how you ever convinced Mr. Emmett, but let me tell you, you haven't convinced me."

Jennifer rose to her feet. "Why don't you get your court order then? Or am I calling your bluff? If anyone in this house is a fraud—it's you."

Without waiting to hear Leila Dee's rebuttal, Jennifer strode from the room.

The episode had left a foul taste in her mouth. Were they all vultures, fighting over the dead mummified bodies of the Kirkwoods, Hubert smiling, clutching a pipe in the library, Hester laid out in the bedroom? But Jennifer didn't feel that *she* was fighting. She was simply claiming her due. And she was the only one who had gone through legitimate channels from the first, to prove her ownership of Seacliff Pines.

There was something else which had troubled her from the very first; though she had pushed it to the back of her mind. Now, she thought of it again. How had Hester Kirkwood died? Of what? Miss Collingwood had been evasive, and Jennifer, distracted by other things, had not pressed for answers. But she had to have them. It did not seem right to be in Hester's house and to assert her ownership without knowing more about her great-aunt's death.

Miss Collingwood, though, was no more eager to speak of her employer than she had been when Jennifer first arrived. Jennifer found her sitting in the breakfast nook mending a pillow case. "Do you mind if I ask you a few questions?" Jennifer asked, drawing out a chair.

Miss Collingwood looked up, her dark eyes startled. "What . . . what questions?"

"About my Aunt Hester."

"Oh. I . . . I was just going to lie down for a while before getting supper." She started to rise.

"It won't take but a minute," Jennifer urged.

"But I..."

"Just a question or two, and if you don't feel like answering, you needn't."

"All right," she said with a meek acquiescence to the inevitable.

"Was Mrs. Kirkwood in poor health for some time or did she take ill suddenly?"

"She...no..." A frown puckered Miss Collingwood's pale, damp forehead. "She did have high blood pressure the last couple of years."

"Was she seeing a doctor for it?"

"She went up to San Francisco once, just the once, and saw a doctor."

"Who?"

She studied the pillow case for a moment. "I don't know. She said he was a money grubber."

"And after that she had no medical attention whatsoever?" Jennifer asked in disbelief.

"Well...not from a doctor."

"Who then?" Miss Collingwood seemed to shrink even more into herself, and Jennifer felt a pang of guilt. "Who did she see?" Jennifer asked, using a milder tone.

"Mr. Peters."

"The taxidermist?"

"He had some medical learning. I think Mrs. Kirkwood told me, he once wanted to be an animal doctor."

Jennifer leaned back in her chair and bit her lip. "I know this is all painful for you, Miss Collingwood. But I would like to know how my aunt died. And you seem to be the only person who can tell me. How did she die?"

Miss Collingwood squirmed in her chair. She

glanced at the ceiling, at the clock, then brought her eyes to a point over Jennifer's shoulder. "I don't rightly know."

Jennifer studied the housekeeper. Perhaps she didn't know. Or perhaps she was lying. "You said her heart stopped. Was it the result of a car accident, a fall?"

"She died in her bed."

"But that doesn't rule out an accident." Jennifer's patience had become thin again. She had the weird, frustrating feeling that she was dueling with a phantom, that Miss Collingwood, herself, had long ago expired, and that in her place was this equivocating, ghostly shadow. "I don't like to pull every word out of you," Jennifer said. "I would appreciate—*please*, could you give me a short account of how my aunt died?"

Miss Collingwood sighed and with her eyes on the pillow case, said, "She took to her bed one night—said she was feeling poorly. The next morning she wasn't any better, and after Mr. Donaldson—the man who says he's Hubert's grandson—after he left, she asked me to call Mr. Peters." She paused and fidgeted with the needle.

"Well, then?" Jennifer prompted. "Did you call Mr. Peters?"

"I . . . we had a phone, then. I called him, and he came." She swallowed.

"From where? I mean, where does he live?"

"He has his shop about five miles below Seacliff Pines—going toward San Simeon."

"And . . ." Jennifer coaxed.

"He . . . he came out right away. He went upstairs and a half hour later, asked for a glass of water."

"Did you go into the room?"

"No. He said Mrs. Kirkwood was in a bad way. And then around noon, he came down and said she was dead."

"Just like that? You didn't ask what had ailed her, why she had died?"

"I . . . no, I didn't ask."

"And there was no doctor?" Jennifer could not help her astonishment. "Why . . . why that's illegal!"

"Mr. Peters said I wasn't to worry. He'd take care of all the details."

It was wrong, all wrong, suspiciously wrong. She wondered if Mr. Emmett knew the circumstances surrounding Hester's death. Apparently it was Mr. Peters who, in taking care of "all the details," had informed the lawyer, either by letter or telephone. But wouldn't Mr. Emmett, quavery as he was at times, want proof of death? Some official verification? Perhaps Mr. Peters had sent him a death certificate, a phony one, filling it in himself putting cause of death as a stroke or heart failure. Perhaps Hester had really died in that manner.

"Did Mr. Peters remove her body immediately?" Jennifer asked.

"Yes. He took it right away and brought it back a week later."

Such haste, Jennifer thought, such indecent haste. Why?

"How can I reach Mr. Peters?" she asked.

Miss Collingwood stared at Jennifer with blank eyes.

"I'd like to talk to Mr. Peters," Jennifer said.

Two pink spots appeared on Miss Collingwood's

cheeks. She got to her feet without a word and crossing the kitchen, went into the pantry.

Jennifer wondered then if the whole story had been a lie. Not the whole story; there must have been a Mr. Peters—or someone like him—to preserve the body. But had he been at Hester's bedside before she died? Or had he been called in afterwards? The thought that Hester might have been murdered, she pushed aside. It was too dangerous a notion, too frightening.

Jennifer waited a few minutes, thinking Miss Collingwood would emerge from the pantry. When she didn't, Jennifer went in after her.

The pantry was one of those large, old fashioned food storage rooms on the cool side of the house with one high, screened window through which the light filtered dimly. The shelves went from floor to ceiling, and in one corner an old abandoned refrigerator gleamed dully. Miss Collingwood was standing at the far end with her back to Jennifer.

"I didn't mean to doubt your word," Jennifer began, "but I think I ought to straighten things out with Mr. Peters."

Miss Collingwood turned. Her eyes were like living coals. "I never lie," she said. She held a knife in one hand. "I never lie." It was a large, wicked-looking, carving knife, its silver blade twinkling like a monstrous, elongated eye in the uncertain light.

"M...Miss Collingwood..." Jennifer protested feebly.

"I am not a liar," the housekeeper repeated, in cold, controlled fury.

"I never called you one," Jennifer managed to

say. More and more those still waters were giving up unexpected facets of Miss Collingwood's personality. She could hate passionately; she did not like being called a liar; and Jennifer, staring at the knife with trepidation, would not be surprised if under that usually meek exterior lay a capacity for sudden and irrational violence. "I am truly sorry if you misunderstood."

Had she murdered Hester? Miss Collingwood hated Hester and had lived for years under her grinding thumb. Had one act, one word, tipped the scales and been too much? A kitchen knife, a fireplace poker, a few drops of poison in the breakfast coffee, all would have been convenient weapons.

"I'm sorry," Jennifer repeated.

The housekeeper didn't seem to hear. There was a strange, fierce glaze in her eyes; the knife in her hand didn't waver.

Jennifer took a step backward, feeling for the door knob, and inadvertently closed the door instead. She stood in the semi-darkness watching Miss Collingwood like a cat watching a serpent. The silence stretched between them, heavy, like the charged atmosphere before a storm. Quietly, Jennifer began to feel for the door knob again, not daring to turn her back.

A shadow flitted across Miss Collingwood's face and Jennifer heard a step outside. "Hello!" Alex's voice boomed. "Is anyone at home?"

Miss Collingwood reached up and pulled on the string attached to a naked bulb. The light flared harshly, revealing Miss Collingwood's features, expressionless and wooden. She turned her back on Jennifer and began slicing a large loaf of bread.

115

Jennifer quickly opened the door. Alex was standing in the middle of the kitchen, a bulging grocery sack in each arm.

"Been hiding?" he grinned. "Say—you look like you've seen a ghost."

Jennifer gave him an oblique glance and said nothing.

"I've got all kinds of goodies, here," Alex went on affably. "Including a couple of steaks. Share them with me? I'm a great cook..."

"No, thank you," Jennifer said, walking past him, hoping that her trembling knees did not betray her.

Once in her room she locked the door. Then on legs which still seemed weak she went into the bathroom and bathed her face in cold water. Was Miss Collingwood mad? She could see how she might be, living so many years shut up with an eccentric like Hester Kirkwood, in a house like Seacliff Pines. Perhaps the housekeeper and Mr. Peters had been in collusion and together had killed Hester. But what had Mr. Peters to gain by it? He was not mentioned in the will and he, unlike Alex and Leila Dee, had not come forward to make any claim.

The more she thought of it, the more it became muddled in her mind. And it was Mr. Peters who held the key to the mystery. Dare she tackle him alone? There was no one in the house she trusted to accompany her.

But she did have John McGraw.

She threw a light coat over her shoulders, slipped quietly down the stairs and out to the garage.

Leaving the driveway, she turned left and drove

north. Her eyes noted the clumps of wild daisies on the mustard colored cliffs, the sea shimmering in wide swatches of green, blue and pure gold; while her mind still dwelt within the shadows of Seacliff Pines. It seemed so illogical, so unreal, that a house of such sinister aspect could exist under the same sky as the beauty that spread out on either side of her.

The car began its ascent on the hairpin turn which gave a panoramic view of the coastline, one which was very much like the view she had wondered at, on the drive down from Carmel. It seemed so very long ago in retrospect. How excited she had been, how eager to see the house which was soon to be hers!

The car slowed, knocking and coughing as it climbed. She pushed the gas pedal to the floor and pulled out the choke, praying the old heap would make it to the top. She was nearly there when the car went into an unexpected burst of speed, and at the same time Jennifer heard an explosive "pop!"

She fought the wheel as the car suddenly careened wildly, scraping the low guard rail on her left—the fragile, and only, barrier between her and the cliff's edge which dropped straight to the rocky chasm below. Then the car veered, bouncing off the bluff on her right.

Gripped in terror, conscious of the wheels spinning and tires squealing, her heart throbbed in an agony of pain. The tawny hills and the blue sky whirled crazily before her eyes as the car skidded again, finally crashing through the rail. The abrupt halt threw Jennifer forward: Silence sang in her ears. The car seemed to be hanging precariously between heaven and earth while she sat perspiring in terror—the primal terror of falling into nothingness. Her clammy hands still clung to the wheel; her brow was beaded with sweat. She dared not move, dared not breathe. The flick of so much as a fingernail could send the car plunging downward.

She became conscious of a tap-tapping on the right window, and winced. The tapping went on, and moving her head slowly, she saw a young man's face pressed against the glass.

"Are you all right?" she thought he was saying.

"Yes..." she mouthed.

He opened the door, and she closed her eyes in pain, expecting the car to totter, her nerves stretched like taut, humming wires.

"Are you sure?" a masculine voice inquired solicituously. He had a thin, curling moustache and a wispy, blond beard at the end of a pointed chin.

"I'm afraid to move," she whispered.

"It's O.K.," he said.

She slid cautiously over the seat, and the young man helped her out. She clung to him for a few moments, the ground under her feet swaying.

"You got a bad flat there," the young man said.

She brought herself to look at the car, then. The front wheels had gone through the guard rail and were resting two, no more than three, inches from the rim of the abyss; the flat right tire was flabby at the base.

They were joined by another young man who had been watching from a parked van across the road. He was short, stocky, with a head of incredibly frizzy, wild hair. "Lucky you didn't go over," he said.

"Yes," said Jennifer still numb, still feeling shock.

The frizzy haired, young man bent to inspect the gray dusty tire. He took out a small knife, worked something loose from it and handed it to Jennifer. "There's your trouble," he said.

It was a nail, not a rusty nail, but a shiny new one.

"Must have picked it up somewhere," the young man said.

"Yes," said Jennifer, staring at the nail. But she didn't pick it up, her mind protested. She couldn't believe it was an accident, not after her experience in the attic. Someone must have deliberately jammed the nail into the tire, someone who knew that sooner or later she would be driving up that dangerous grade. Through her mind flashed a picture of the garage, of Alex shoving tools, rags, and little jars of tacks and nails aside. And she thought too, how his eyes could change swiftly into a dangerous, dark, dark blue.

"I am not a gentleman," he had once told her.

Had it been a warning?

CHAPTER IX

Together the two young men pushed Jennifer's car around the corner, onto a graveled ledge and changed the tire for her. She offered to pay them, but they refused. She thanked them profusely, shaking their hands, telling them how grateful she was that they had come along.

After they had driven off, she got into her own car. "Yes," she thought, "I am lucky, lucky to be alive." She closed her eyes against the picture which rose in her mind; but it was there all the same, vivid against her eyelids: the car flying into space, bouncing, crashing down the steep slope of the rocky gorge, finally exploding into a burst of flame.

Could people get murdered because of a house? Taking a tissue from her purse, she wiped her damp hands and then the steering wheel. She wondered if Seacliff Pines was that valuable. Value was in the eye of the beholder, she told herself. To Miss Collingwood Seacliff Pines, for all its miserable memories, was the only home she had known for most of her adult life. To Alex, who said he was a writer, the house probably represented more money than he could earn in a long time. And to Leila Dee, in her pink negligee, it offered security, a haven for old age. And what of herself, Jennifer Sargent? Yes, the house was going to be her ticket to freedom, a new life. But she could not in her wildest imagination see herself harming anyone, let alone *killing* for Seacliff Pines.

Was someone really trying to murder her?

A station wagon went by, and from its rear window, a young child waved, the sound of happy, high laughter reaching her on the wind.

With a convulsive movement Jennifer started the car and released the brake. It was futile and senseless to dwell on the morbidity of catastrophe, murder. It was a waste of time. She gripped the wheel firmly as she went winding and twisting down the grade. From a wholly logical and factual standpoint what proof did she have that an attempt had been made on her life? Maybe that blow on her shoulder, in the attic had been caused by a protruding object she had brushed against in her haste. As for Miss Collingwood in the pantry, she had to admit, honestly, that the woman had not actually threatened her. She had looked angry, but she had not threatened her. The knife in her hand just happened to be there because she was preparing to slice bread. And the nail in the tire? Was that so unusual? But deep down in the innermost core of her heart, Jennifer's uneasiness remained.

Some three minutes later Jennifer reached John McGraw's driveway. Bumping down in between fields of brown and flagged weeds, she saw that John's car was gone. Disappointment dragged at her. More than ever she felt the need to talk to someone who would not scoff at her suspicions, someone she could trust.

She sighed and with an effort, pulled herself up out of her mental funk, turned the car around and drove out. Instead of going back to the house, she went into Torrey. There, leafing through the local telephone directory, she found the listing for *Whitlock Peters, Taxidermist.* She dialed the number and after the phone rang several times, she was told that service for Mr. Peters had been disconnected.

"Why?" she wondered. "Had he moved?" Nevertheless, she copied his address in her little green book.

Dutch, the storekeeper, was busy with a customer, a man in high boots and corduroy jacket. They were discussing the relative merits of two fishing reels, and she waited patiently until they were through. "Do you know a Mr. Peters?" Jennifer asked, catching Dutch as he turned away from the man.

"Mr. Peters...?" He adjusted the pencil behind his ear. "Old Whit, you mean? The taxidermist? Haven't seen him for quite a while. Nothing unusual in that. He's sort of retired. A shy man, keeps to himself."

"His phone is disconnected," Jennifer said. "Do you remember when you last saw him?"

"Oh—let me see. Ellen...!" He turned his head and called down the counter where his wife, a thin, pretty woman, was helping a young girl on with a straw sun hat. "When did old Whit come in last?"

"Oh," she said, thinking a moment. "Must have been way before summer. Last May. Said he was going on a little trip."

"There," said Dutch, turning back to her. "Although you never know with him. He might have come back. You got something you want mounted? There's another man does that work in Carmel, not as good as old Whit..."

"I'll keep it in mind," said Jennifer, and then as an afterthought, "What does Mr. Peters look like?"

"He's a little man, can't be any more than five feet, two, give or take an inch. He's about seventy, salt and pepper hair, small beard and bowlegged as a cowboy. Why d'you ask?"

"Just curious," said Jennifer.

Jennifer left the cool dimness of the general store and went out into the dancing afternoon sunshine, carrying in her mind a picture of Mr. Peters. He did not sound like an ogre; he could be capable of deceit, but not murder.

She had almost reached the rusted gates of Seacliff Pines when she decided on impulse to go on and look up Mr. Peters. What harm could a small, seventy year old man do to her? And she was curious; no, more than curious. It seemed to her that if she could solve the mystery of her aunt's death, she would have one less anxiety to deal with. Perhaps, Mr. Peters could help in clearing away some of her doubts and suspicions. He might know about Miss Leila Dee, about Alex; perhaps he could shed some light on Hester's will, a will which was beginning to seem more and more strange.

After a few miles she slowed the car, checking her speedometer from time to time. The sun dimmed, then disappeared behind the fog, slowly spreading in from the sea. She rolled up the windows, thought briefly of turning back, but just as quickly, dismissed the idea. She was almost there; she could tell by the numbers on the boxes.

She nearly passed it when she saw a mailbox on her left, topped by a metal woodpecker bleached to a scabrous pink, announcing WHITLOCK PETERS in white, blurred letters. Beyond it was a dirt drive barred by a padlocked chain that sagged between two gray, worm eaten posts. The drive, leading up into the high hills, disappeared beneath low hanging trees.

Jennifer drove her car up to the chain, got out, and locked the doors. Then skirting one of the posts, she began to climb. Under the great, branch spread wild oaks, it was cool. Birds twittered and called over her head. She heard the sound of running water and presently caught a glimpse of a stream gurgling busily over smooth, dark gray stones.

Ascending higher she emerged from the trees into a sun drenched field where withered mallow and blown thistles rustled in the tall, sered grass. Turning to look back she saw the wide band of fog below, hiding the water, and closer, her car, parked like a squat beetle at the base of the drive.

Up ahead was a house built of redwood, cantilevered into the hill with one large expanse of glass under an overhang. The house surprised her. She had pictured "Old Whit," the recluse, the small, shy elderly man living in a hermit's hut, something humble, perhaps tacked together of old lumber and discarded crates. But this house, though not large, had design, if not style and flair. The only thing which fitted in with her preconceived notion was its remoteness from the highway.

As she approached, she was struck by the utter stillness surrounding the house. The shrill insect song which had accompanied her across the field was silenced, the wind hushed; even her footsteps were muffled by the soft, sandy soil. The house, rising above her on stilts, its stark profile angled toward the sea, had the air of an abandoned ship, becalmed, mysterious, inaccessible.

124

She found a staircase around the back where the weeds grew waist high, some coming through the cracks in the wooden stairs. She had her foot on the bottom step when suddenly she heard a peculiar knocking sound, the sound of wood hitting wood.

Thud—thud—thud. A long pause. Thud—thud—thud.

Was the old man at home after all? She went up the stairs to a tree shaded porch. The blank faced door held a knocker in its center, a brass replica of a squat snouted bulldog's head. She lifted it gingerly and then let it fall. The brassy echo startled a lizard who darted across the porch and disappeared over the side.

Thud—thud—thud. Pause. Thud—thud—thud.

"Hello!" she called, her voice drowning in the eerie silence. "Is anyone at home?"

The dull thud, thud, thud, answered her.

A cold little wind moved in the branches overhead. Thud—thud—thud. Pause. Thud—thud—thud. Jennifer shivered. She went along the porch and turning a corner saw a large empty bird cage suspended from a beam of the overhang. The wind stirred it, and it swung against the house. Thud, thud, thud.

A bird cage.

Some of the tension went out of her. She looked around. An old lawn mower was leaning against the tree trunk. From the looks of the overgrown, dried weeds, it had not been used in a long time. A coiled water hose lay beside it like a green serpent asleep in the sun. Running along the porch railing was a shelf lined with flowerpots. The flowers, petunias, were all withered now.

Heavy curtains had been drawn across the one large floor-to-ceiling window opening out to the porch. She found a gap in the center of the curtains and peering through, she recoiled in shock at a single fierce eye which gazed back at her.

Mr. Peters? Had he been watching all this time? Going from window to window, following her every movement?

But she hadn't *done* anything, she told herself, except peek through the window. The eye, however, had stared at her in unblinking accusation. It was a large eye, very large, not the eye of a small man, five feet-two. It came to her then that Mr. Peters was a taxidermist, and with a half hysterical laugh in her throat, she pressed her face to the glass again. It was just as she had guessed. The eye belonged to a stuffed owl.

Standing on tiptoe and craning her neck, she was able to get a narrow, tunneled view of the room beyond the bird. From what she could see, it was empty; bare walls, bare floor, dust moted sunshine, a shut door on the farthest side. Except for the owl there wasn't the slightest clue of occupancy.

Above her the empty cage spun in the wind, thumping against the house. Sunlight filtering down through the tree's leaves made spattered patterns along the curtained window. Suddenly a large shadow wheeled across Jennifer's vision, and she turned quickly.

There was nothing but the lawnmower, the tree, the coiled hose.

The remoteness, the loneliness of the house, struck her with new force. She hurried along the porch, descending the stairs with a clatter. The thin wind sighed and whispered, the grassy slope bent as if hidden footsteps were trodding over it. For one horrible moment Jennifer felt trapped, betrayed; her car on the road below miles away seemed impossible to reach.

She forced her legs to carry her around the house, across the field. She did not look behind. But she had a vague sensation that shadows were following her, dodging her footsteps. When she reached the trees, the shadows seemed to spring up on all sides of her, and she began to run. Not until she slid down the last few yards of the embankment to her car did she draw an easy breath.

The fog was coming in fast, wafting in long, opaque fingers across the road. Already the trees and mailboxes on the other side were lost in mist. She quickly unlocked the car, slid under the wheel and pulled the door shut.

Her search for Mr. Peters had only heightened the mystery. Whether "Old Whit" had vanished willingly, or unwillingly, she did not know. But he was gone, had been gone, perhaps "since last May," as the storekeeper's wife had said. Where? Why? His departure had coincided with Hester's death. Mr. Peters must have left just after he had finished preparing Hester's body. Had he run away? Gone on a trip? Perhaps he was visiting a relative, a friend. Perhaps even now, he was reading a newspaper or drinking a cup of coffee or window shopping on a busy street somewhere, totally unaware Hester's death had caused such uneasiness, such a stir at Seacliff Pines.

Yet suppose he had never left. In her mind's eye she saw the vacant room, the shadow wheeling across the curtain, the empty bird cage, felt the chill wind and heard the grass rustle. Had something happened to Mr. Peters, something unforeseen and unpleasant?

Apparently he was the only one who knew how Hester had died. And if she had been murdered—not by his hand, but by another's—then Mr. Peters shared a very dangerous secret with someone, a someone who might have found it necessary to silence the little taxidermist permanently.

Ought she to inform Mr. Emmett? But what could she say? There wasn't a single fact she could present to the lawyer to support her suspicions, not one piece of evidence to arouse his serious interest.

When she reached Seacliff Pines and drove into the garage, Alex's car was there, red, sassy, sleek, an insolent reminder of his presence. She wondered how much *he* knew of Hester's death. According to Miss Collingwood, he had left the house on the morning Hester had come down with her fatal illness. Had he anything to do with it? And, if so, why had he waited seven months to come back to Seacliff Pines?

She sat for a few minutes studying the red car. The window was rolled down. She opened her door, squeezed out and took a quick look beyond the garage door. Then she slipped her hand through the window and opened Alex's glove compartment. Feeling like a criminal, her heart beating fast, she drew out an envelope. It was addressed to Mr. Alex Donaldson. *Donaldson.*

Kirkwood, my foot!

If she could find the car registration that would be proof incontrovertible. Her hand went back to the glove compartment when suddenly she thought she heard a step along the driveway. Blushing with guilt, she hurriedly closed the compartment, and turned back to her own car pretending to be busy inspecting the tire.

Footsteps crunched on the gravel, and a shadow appeared on the fender above her. "Having trouble?" Alex asked amiably.

She got slowly to her feet. Had he seen her riffling through the glove compartment? "No. Not now. I had a flat a while back." She watched his face closely.

"That can be bad on the Coast Highway."

"It was. But I was lucky." Had he been spying on her, keeping track of her coming and going from an upstairs window?

"You ought to have that old wreck gone over. I'll do it for you, if you like."

"No, thanks. John's looked at it," she lied. Well, it was half a lie. He had recharged the battery. She knew one thing. She didn't want Alex tinkering with her car.

"It was a nail," she said. "A shiny nail in the tire."

"They can be bad."

"I must have picked it up here, in the garage."

He studied her for a long moment. "Did it have my name on it?" he asked, and suddenly smiled.

"Of course," she replied flippantly, and turning, went out.

She unlocked the front door and crossing the threshold was enfolded at once by the house's quiet dimness. Again she was struck by the eerie way Seacliff Pines absorbed all sound, all noise, except that of its own making. One would never know that five people were living and breathing under its roof. Wood paneled walls and thick carpets and high ceilings must have had something to do with it. Had it been Hubert's design to have a home where voices sounded hushed, where movement

129

was barely discernible, where the house made its own conversation? It was doubtful; Hubert's portrait in the library showed too merry an eye, too affable and friendly a face. Bad taste he might have had, but it was unlikely he would have been happy living in the gloomy atmosphere of a tomb-like house. No, Seacliff Pines had probably acquired its secretive air over the thirty years since his death, falling into neglect through Hester's frugality, gathering dust and shadows, permeated with the hostility shared by two women living out their days in mutual distrust.

Once in her room Jennifer removed her sweater and shoes and lay down on the bed. Pain needled behind her eyes and she closed them. She heard the tap-tap of a tree branch on the window and that curious, jangling sound, but she ignored it and felt everything recede from her conscious mind as she dropped off to sleep.

She awoke to darkness. Glancing at her watch she was surprised to see that it was only five o'clock. She thought she had been sleeping for hours. Swinging her legs over the side of the bed, she heard the creak of a board and the sound of soft footsteps in the corridor. Her door which she had forgotten to lock, was partially opened and looking through it she saw Alex pass. Even in that brief glimpse, she had noted that he was shoeless. Curious, Jennifer crept out. He was walking carefully as if he were trying to muffle the sound of his step.

It was almost pitch black in the hallway, but Jennifer, guided by the gleam of Alex's white shirt, followed him at what she hoped was a safe distance. She felt somewhat melodramatic, tiptoeing after Alex like a comic detective in an old, silent movie, but curiosity drew her on.

The white patch ahead of her disappeared as Alex had turned the corner at the end of the corridor. She went on and reaching the point where Alex had vanished, she paused, her eyes straining through the darkness.

Suddenly a penciled ray of light broke through the darkness, sweeping the ceiling and wall. She shrank into a shadowed doorway, pressing her back against the cold wood. The light lingered for a few heart splitting seconds, inches from her feet, and then went out.

She began to sweat, her ears aching as she listened for the returning pad of footsteps. But the only sound that was heard was the distant, complaining groan of a floor board. She bent her head forward and saw a glimmer of light on the attic staircase. Alex was going up into the turret. She waited until she heard the faint click of a closing door. Then silently, on careful feet, she made her way back to her room.

Alex was searching for something, going over the house secretly, that much was obvious. But what was it he hoped to find. Money. She remembered him saying, "The old gal must have plenty stashed away." He had worked closely with Hester for a number of months, and although, according to him, she had not given him all the information he needed; he must have had more than one hint which led him to surmise she was wealthy. Jennifer herself looked upon the idea skeptically, almost scornfully—the time worn myth of a recluse hoarding gold beneath the floor boards.

But suppose Alex believed it?

And Leila Dee? Suppose she (a woman who did not strike Jennifer as the type avidly keen on retiring in the country) wanted Seacliff Pines precisely because she thought money was concealed within its walls?

And Miss Collingwood, did she think the same?

Did all three of them share this dream, this myth, the promise of a miser's hoard?

And Jennifer, whose claim to sole ownership of Seacliff Pines was the strongest, stood in their way.

CHAPTER X

Surprisingly, for all her anxiety, Jennifer slept well that night and in the morning her mind, refreshed, turned to mundane matters like groceries. They were completely out of milk and eggs. She hopped out of bed and opened the bedroom curtains. Outside the fog curled like white smoke along the drive. Jennifer considered waiting another hour before she went into Torrey, but looking through the window, she could see the mist thinning in the tree tops. Hopefully, the fog would be no problem during the drive.

She had gone a half-mile from the house when she became conscious of a car following her. At first she reasoned that it was some driver unsure of the road, made even more timid by poor visibility. But as the minutes went by, she became more and more uneasy. Coming to a wide space in the road, she pulled over and stopped. The mist that had not cleared as she hoped, rose like vapors of steam from the pavement, and for a short time her view in the side mirror was obscured. But then a torn hole in the curtain of fog revealed the car behind. It had stopped too.

The hole became larger and she saw the car clearly now. It was Leila Dee's dusty, white Ford. She could just make out the short figure at the wheel—Charlie.

What was he up to? Had he been sent by Leila Dee to follow her?

Fear gripped her as she thought of the hairpin turns ahead, the yawning chasms, the narrow road with only a few inches to spare for two cars side by side. She considered turning back but the sun had broken through the fog on the road ahead; whereas behind her the fog still lingered. It was too dangerous to turn back.

She started the car and shot out onto the highway. She had only two miles to go before she reached the store. There was no traffic, absolutely none, not even a camper or truck. She threw a quick glance at the mirror. Charlie was close behind. She prayed for a car to overtake them, for a hitchhiker beside the road. But the unwinding landscape ahead was empty of the slightest sign of humanity. Down she drove, following the macadam ribbon over a stone bridge, through a parting of great rocks, and up over a knoll. There were no side roads, no driveways, no houses. It was as if she were on an endless highway to nowhere.

Charlie wouldn't be so close on her heels unless he had a purpose, a dangerous purpose. What did he want? Was he planning to force her over the side? Only this morning she had caught him peering at her from behind the clothes rack in the entry hall as she had locked the door to her room. But then she had ignored him.

She wanted to stop, but she was more afraid of that than she was of going on. The road started to ascend again, up and up, disappearing around the base of a cliff. Her sweaty hands gripped the wheel, and she gritted her teeth as she forced the rackety engine forward. Charlie was gaining on her. She knew it; she could feel it. He was going to ram her over the edge when they got to the top. She reached the summit and with wheels screeching, rounded the bend, dashing down the hill and around the next turn. "My God," she thought, "what if the brakes give out?"

Charlie was sticking to her like a burr. But he wasn't gaining anymore. Perhaps Leila Dee's old Ford couldn't get up enough speed. The thought cheered her, but not much. One more curve at the speed of the last one, and she wouldn't need Charlie's help to go over the edge. She took the next—and final—turn more slowly, her heart clamoring painfully, not daring to look in the rear view mirror. A minute later the gray buildings of Torrey came into view.

She parked the car, her whole body trembling, and wiped the perspiration from her hands and face. She saw the Ford shoot past, brake, then make a wide U-turn and come back toward her. Quickly, she got out of the car and went into the cool, safe bustle of the store.

She was getting eggs out of the refrigerated case when, from the corner of her eye, she saw Charlie idling over the magazine rack. She hesitated, then went up to him boldly.

"Charlie," she began without preamble, "you were following me. Why?"

He shifted his cigar from one side of his mouth to the other. "I had to get a couple of things for Leila, and I thought you might be headin' for the store. I didn't know the way."

"Know the way?" she asked incredulously. "You can't miss it."

"I can," he said matter-of-factly. "I ain't no good

at findin' places. And, lady..." He took the cigar out of his mouth. "...lady, I gotta tell you somethin'. You drive like a maniac."

She stared at him. He didn't seem like a violent person. Maybe he was telling the truth. But it was safer not to trust him, not to trust anybody. If she were removed than Leila Dee's chances for acquiring Seacliff Pines would be that much better. Any one of the claimant's chances would be better.

"Please don't follow me on the way home," Jennifer told Charlie. "It makes me very nervous."

He promised not to, but did anyway—though at a more discreet distance.

That afternoon John came over to suggest a walk on the beach. but Jennifer who had for days been wanting to clear the underbrush from the brick walk skirting the house, prevailed upon him to join her. While they were hunting down garden tools in the garage, she told him how she had gone to look for Mr. Peters.

"So you wanted to find him because you thought Hester was...was *murdered*?"

It did sound a little far fetched, she had to admit. "But don't you think it was funny she didn't have a doctor?"

"No. She was an old lady—stingy, from what you tell me—and a recluse. I'd think it funny if she *did* have a doctor."

She decided not to tell him about the flat tire, or about Charlie following her. He might think her odd, someone who saw threat written on everyone's face, someone who imagined the whole world was against her.

They found a couple of pairs of shears, passably

136

useful, and a saw and some old gloves for Jennifer. Beginning at the front of the house, they attacked the matted growth of vines and bushes, grown old and tough with neglect, choked with years of accumulated, rotting pine needles. It was hard going but they hacked away, cheerfully, chopping through knotted ropes of ivy, pulling out great handfuls of weeds. It gave Jennifer a sense of accomplishment to see the mossy bricks beneath, uncover one by one. And it took her mind off the inhabitants of Seacliff Pines.

They had been working for over an hour when Jennifer got to her feet. "What are we going to do with this mess?" she asked, surveying the dead greenery heaped on the driveway.

"Shovel it in boxes," John said, "and cart them off to the dump."

"Boxes," she said, creasing her brow. "There might be some empties in the attic."

"Why don't I get them?"

"O.K. The staircase is at the end of the second floor corridor."

Jennifer went on clipping and snipping. She had been working on her knees; but now, to give them a rest, she crouched on her heels. Pulling up a massed tangle of roots, she unearthed a long, pale snake and suddenly recoiling, fell backward. Simultaneously a large object plummeted downward from above, crashing into a thousand fragments where her head had been only a second earlier.

The blood drained from her cheeks as she stared at pieces of white, blue and brown plaster. It had been a statue of a peasant girl, one of the many scattered throughout the house. Not heavy itself, it would be lethal when dropped from a height. She thought she heard a window closing and glanced quickly upward. Blank faced, the odd sized, curtained windows of the Pines met her gaze, sneering at her in smug glee.

She got to her feet and ran up the stairs and into the house which, as usual, was silent as a tomb. But Jennifer knew they were all at home. Jennifer thought of them, boiling with anger; Alex, Miss Collingwood, Leila Dee, Charlie, all had become enemies. One of them had aimed that statue at her, and she meant to find the guilty party. She was starting up the staircase when suddenly the heavy silence was ripped apart by a blood curdling scream. She paused, her hand on the rail, her anger momentarily forgotten. A door slammed and there was the sound of running footsteps.

She continued upward and when she reached the landing she heard Charlie shouting, "I ain't staying, I tell you! I ain't staying." He was in Leila Dee's room and the door was open. "A house with a stiff in it...!"

So Charlie had found Hester, Jennifer thought with a grim smile.

Leila murmured something, and Charlie's voice cut her off. "The whole idea was nutty. I told you..."

John McGraw, coming down from the attic, his arms full of boxes, met Jennifer at Leila's door. "What happened?"

"I know what happened to *him*," Jennifer said. "What I want to find out..." Charlie and Leila were looking at them, Charlie caught in mid-sentence, Leila lounging on the chaise. "Someone," Jennifer said, entering the room, "tossed a statue at me from a window up here."

138

They both looked at her in surprise, an amaze-
ment so genuine that Jennifer found it hard to
believe it was false.

John said, "My God! Are you hurt?"

"No, it missed me," Jennifer said. "But just."
Then turning to Leila Dee and Charlie. "You
didn't...?"

"Of course we didn't," Leila Dee interrupted,
irritably. "You got a nerve barging in here and
accusing us of some dumb thing. What was it?
Somebody threw a vase at you?" She snorted.

"Nutty, I tell you," Charlie began, "Nutty..."

Jennifer went down to the kitchen with John
trailing behind her. Alex and Miss Collingwood
were there and when asked, they both denied any
knowledge of the falling statue, Alex giving
Jennifer a peculiar, appraising look.

"Maybe," said John as they went outside to the
brick walk, "the window was open and a curtain,
blowing in the wind, knocked it over."

"I could have sworn I heard a window closing,"
she said, "And when I looked up they were all
shut." But could she be sure? She had been upset,
her upward glance cursory.

"It wasn't me," said John.

"I know," she said. "Let's get this mess in boxes.
I think I've lost my appetite for gardening."

She lay for a long time that night worrying
about the broken statue, wondering who might
have tossed it at her from the window, wondering
if maybe John had been right and it had fallen just
before Charlie or someone else had closed a
window. Sometime, during the restless night, she
heard a car start up and thought it might be Alex

139

who had decided to drive up to the Lodge. But when she came downstairs at ten o'clock the next morning, she was informed by Alex that it had been Charlie who had left in the night.

"He left a message for Leila," Alex said. "A message in lurid language, the gist of which was that she could have Seacliff Pines, but he was going back to civilization."

"Have you told her?"

"She isn't up. But I don't think she'll be happy. It was her car, I understand."

"Maybe she'll leave too," Jennifer said.

But it was a futile hope. When Leila Dee was informed of Charlie's departure she was furious with him and swore she'd get even with him, swore she'd call the police. But she never made an attempt to do either.

For the most part she kept to her room, and Jennifer rarely saw her. Leila had made some sort of arrangement with Miss Collingwood, whereby the housekeeper prepared her meals—a noon brunch and a late dinner—on trays, and Leila would come down the stairs to fetch them. Somehow, she had coaxed Alex into shopping for her, and he would bring home brown paper sacks of wines and snacks and Leila's favorite brand of cigarettes from the general store at Torrey. Privately, Alex thought Leila a fraud and a joke. To Jennifer this seemed like the pot calling the kettle black and she said so, a statement Alex smilingly ignored.

After Charlie's departure there followed a week of gray gloom, the morning mists giving way to lowering, slate colored skies. It was depressing weather, and Jennifer felt it most keenly when she was in the house. There the scowling woodwork and dim corridors lent themselves to black thoughts and silent brooding. Climbing the staircase or sitting in her room, she was convinced that the three of them, Leila Dee, Alex and Miss Collingwood, together or singularly, were bent on destroying her. But once away from Seacliff Pines in the company of John McGraw or driving the highway to the general store where she could lose herself in the clatter and talk of everyday people, she saw her situation differently. They were not going to really hurt her or to kill her, nothing as extreme, as dramatic as that. It was going to be— was already—a battle of nerves by which they hoped eventually to squeeze her out. Then they would probably turn on one another.

Well, she refused to be beaten. Though she never spoke of her deepest fears to John, she came to lean on him more and more, and when he told her he would be away for a week—a ceramics show in San Francisco—she knew she would miss him. She had offered to look after his dog during his absence, but he had already arranged with a neighbor's boy to feed Rena and run her twice a day, on the beach.

One day, to her surprise, Jennifer found Rena at the front door, barking and whining and scratching to be let in. Jennifer surmised that Rena had jumped the fence and gone in search of her master. She brought the dog into the house where she stood in the entry hall, a shag rug on four legs, wagging a stumpy tail, her fur damp and steaming from the thick fog outside. Thinking Rena was hungry, Jennifer led her into the kitchen and fed her two cans of corned-beef hash which she demolished in four convulsive gulps. Then, not knowing what else to do with her, Jennifer took Rena up to her bedroom.

The decision was a mistake. Rena couldn't seem to settle down. She prowled the room, and sniffing and grunting she finally scratched open the door, running out into the hall. A moment later she began to bark.

Jennifer ran out to her. The dog was sitting at Hester's door, head lifted in the darkness, voicing her displeasure to the frowning ceiling above.

A door slammed open and Leila Dee in her pink negligee appeared in a shaft of light. "Get that damned dog out of here!" she ordered. "It gives me the creeps."

Jennifer grabbed Rena by the collar and pulled her down the stairs. She opened the front door. "There you go. Out!"

Rena sat down on her rump and refused to budge.

"Having trouble?" Alex's voice came out of nowhere.

Jennifer's pulse jumped as she let go of the dog. Alex was standing behind her on the bottom step of the staircase. She wondered why she hadn't heard his approach until she noticed he wasn't wearing shoes. "Where did you come from?" she asked.

"My half of the house," he answered, smiling. "Your boyfriend's dog?"

"Yes..."

"Doesn't want to go out, does he?" Then to the dog he said, "Come on, let's go, boy."

"It's a girl," she said testily.

"Come on girl." He went out onto the porch and whistled softly.

Rena got up off her haunches and padded across the threshold. "Sit!" said Alex. Rena obediently lowered her furry bulk, stretching out on the wooden boards of the veranda, her head between her paws.

Alex came in and closed the door. "You see how simple it is" he said, "when you have a way with females?"

Jennifer gave him a look which she hoped conveyed her full scorn.

"Except with you," he went on pleasantly. "I don't seem to have much luck with you. In fact, I have a feeling..."

"It's probably right, whatever it is," she said, cutting him short, and starting toward the stairs.

He caught her arm, not roughly, but with a slight encirclement of the fingers. But it frightened Jennifer, and she had enough insight to realize that her fright this time, at least, had little to do with their disagreement over Seacliff Pines. It was his touch which suddenly disturbed her, an electrifying touch, bringing the blood to her face, flooding her with a tide of emotion that she had been unaware of until now. It was not only frightening, but bewildering, too. She had thought of herself as fairly sophisticated, a pretty girl who was quite accustomed to men's advances, always in control. But Alex's physical effect on her was devastating. And he knew it. She could tell by the pinpoints of amusement in his eyes, by the slight curl of his mouth. That was what made him all the more hateful.

"Don't touch me." She wrenched her arm free.

He did not move, did not speak. She could not bring herself to look at his face, but she felt his

143

closeness and sensed that his gaze was unsmiling now.

She turned as his hand dropped away and started up the stairs.

"No compromise?" she heard him say.

"None." She kept on going.

"You might lose it all," he warned.

"I don't intend to," she said. She knew he was still standing at the foot of the stairs watching her until she disappeared into her room. There were so many things she wished she could ask him. What was he looking for? Why did he prowl about the house in stockinged feet with a flashlight? Had he tried to knock her unconscious in the attic, put a nail in her tire?

As she began to undress for bed she heard Rena barking and whimpering down below. But by the time she crawled between the sheets and extinguished her light, Rena had ceased to complain. Either she had given in to sleep or had decided to return home.

Hours later Jennifer awoke to the solemn tolling of the hall clock in the entry below. One, two, three, she counted, three o'clock. Her eyelids flickered with drowsiness, yet something, a curious uneasiness, kept her eyes from shutting completely. She hated the house at night. It was the worst time for her, a time when her fancy took flight, when she gave sinister meaning to every sound, every tick, every creak, when even the silences seemed ominous. She rolled over on her stomach, pressing her face into the pillow, and the next moment she was instantly alert. Her heart began to trip and hammer in her ears. Someone was in the room! She felt a presence, a secret presence concealed in the shadows just beyond the foot of the bed.

But it *couldn't* be possible. She had locked the door. It was the first thing she had done when she came upstairs. Instinctively, she felt it was important to remain perfectly still and feign sleep. But her heart beat so wildly that she was sure it could be heard.

Cautiously she slit open one eye. She thought she saw a darker shadow outlined against the gray curtains. Was it moving and coming toward her. A soft, shuffling sound caught her ear and her mouth went dry. She wanted to scream, but she couldn't. It was as if every muscle had shrunk, shriveled, her bones crumbling to ash, and she had been left only with that savage, painful heartbeat.

An eternity passed while she died over and over again. She felt something brush the bed, and she quickly squeezed her eyes shut. Someone was bending over her. She could hear breathing, the soft intake and outgo of air. An image formed itself in the retina of her closed eyes, a huge bird of prey with black, spreading wings and sharp, curved beak. She met death once again in her mind as she imagined that sharp beak knifing her between the shoulder blades. Or would there be hands choking the life from her? A pillow, perhaps, would come down and smother her. A bubble formed in her aching lungs. If she were to die, she couldn't allow it with her eyes shut, without knowing or seeing. Summoning a death-defying courage, she opened her eyes, and with one lightning movement, turned over and sat up.

A current of air stirred the heavy brocade curtains. The clock downstairs tick-tocked on its ponderous journey. There was no one standing over the bed, no one at its foot. She turned her head. The door, as she had surmised from the sounds of the clock, was open. But, again, she asked herself how it could be, when she remembered distinctly closing and locking it?

Her hand, trembling as if struck by palsy, reached out across the blanket for the bedside lamp and touched something soft and cold. Her fingers did not linger but found the switch and the light blinked on, throwing nebulous shadows on to the walls. Biting her lip, she turned her eyes downward.

Sick horror gagged her. There lying beside her on the night stand was a hand. It was a woman's hand. It wore topaz rings on the fingers which were yellow; the nails were painted red. Around its wrist were two bracelets. Hester's disembodied hand lay there in terrifying reality.

With a curious detachment, she heard herself scream.

CHAPTER XI

She must have negotiated the stairs somehow, but she had no recollection of doing so. She only remembered finding herself leaning against the double glass doors in the entry hall, her hair hanging over her eyes. She was gasping, sobbing to gain control.

A light went on behind her. "Miss Sargent?" Her name came to her in a frightened whisper.

Biting her lip, Jennifer turned. Miss Collingwood was standing to the right of the staircase, her dark eyes, the only color in an ash gray face. She was wearing a brown plaid bathrobe over her nightdress. That and her hair braided in a thin rope down her back gave her the look of a frightened child.

"What is it?" Miss Collingwood whispered.

"I..." Jennifer shuddered, thinking of the yellow, curling fingers. They recalled a horror film of her childhood in which the hand of a murdered man refused to remain buried with his corpse. "In...in my room...a hand."

It seemed that Miss Collingwood's face went even whiter. "Mrs. Kirkwood's?" Her eyes were deep pits of fear.

"Yes...I...someone must have put it there to frighten me." But it baffled her how they could with the door locked. Unless, she had just *assumed* she had locked the door?

"*She* put it there," Miss Collingwood said, her eyes rolling upward toward the stairs.

"No," said Jennifer firmly; though in her mind she wasn't sure. She would never be sure of anything again.

"She cut off her own hand and put it there," Miss Collingwood went on in a low, intense voice. "But she won't come downstairs. Hubert won't let her come downstairs."

Jennifer took a step forward. "Miss Collingwood . . ."

Behind her the front door opened and Alex came in. "Who screamed?" he asked. Jennifer stared at him, speechless. He was fully clothed, even in shoes, and he was carrying a flashlight. The clock clanged the half-hour. "Was it you, Jenny?" he asked.

"You heard me *outside*?" Jennifer asked. It was three-thirty; why was Alex out walking in the fog at three-thirty in the morning?

"Yes—it was enough to wake the dead."

Miss Collingwood gasped.

"Leila Dee didn't hear me," Jennifer said, looking up the staircase. Was he telling the truth? Had he been out of the house? Perhaps he had slipped quietly through the door the moment she had made her gruesome discovery and began to scream.

"Miss Dee takes sleeping pills," Alex said. "She claims, she never hears a sound." He smiled. "Aren't you going to tell me what happened?" His amused eyes glanced over her, and she realized suddenly that in her terrified haste, she had come downstairs without her robe. Only a flimsy, thin strapped nightgown stood between her and nakedness.

A gentleman would keep his eyes from roving. But, then, Alex himself had admitted he wasn't a gentleman. She lifted her chin. It was better to ignore him. Let him look. She wasn't going to make a complete fool of herself by running off like a prude, blushing with shame.

Miss Collingwood said, "She saw Mrs. Kirkwood's hand."

"*What*?" Alex exclaimed.

"I..." Jennifer began, forgetting her anger at the memory of those ghoulish yellow fingers, "I saw..." How could she say it? "Someone cut off Hester's hand and put it in my bed."

"You mean the hand of the...?" he asked, surprised.

"Yes," she said hurriedly. Was he acting a role of concern and shocked innocence? She challenged him. "Come and see," she said, "if you don't believe me."

She started up the stairs, glancing over her shoulder to make sure Alex was following. She went into her room and slipped into the robe which was lying at the foot of the bed. "It's there on the end table," she said, gesturing as Alex came through the door. She did not want to look at it again.

"There's nothing here," Alex said.

She approached the bed. The lamp threw its rays in a circle of roseate light over the bedside table and the tumbled bedclothes. The hand was gone.

"It was here," said Jennifer in a wooden voice.

"It was here only a few minutes ago." She strode to the wall and switched on the overhead light. Her eyes raked the bed and the floor. She lifted the blankets and looked between the sheets. "It was here," she muttered. Getting down on her knees, she searched underneath the bed, her fingers finding only velvety fluff and dust.

"Maybe..." Alex began.

"No," she said, rising from the floor. "It was here!" Stripping the blanket from the bed, she shook it out. But the hand was gone, vanished into thin air.

"Maybe you had a nightmare," Alex concluded, without the sarcasm Jennifer had expected.

"No—I wasn't dreaming. I couldn't have been more wide awake." She tightened the sash of her robe. "I woke up when the clock was striking. The door was open. I thought I had locked it. I knew someone was in the room; I felt it, someone standing over me, breathing..." Her eyes flew to his face. He looked quickly down at the carpet, studying its intricate pattern.

"Was it you?" Jennifer asked.

"Of course not," he said, meeting her gaze.

"You don't believe me, then."

"Well, there's one good way to see if you've been dreaming or not." He started from the room, then turned. "You might as well come along too. I'm sure you won't take my word for it.

Hester's room smelled of antiseptic and mold. Alex clicked on the light, one dim bulb under a shaded wall lamp. Hester's body lay stiff and solid, toes and nose pointing toward the ceiling, a visible reminder of her omnipotent presence at Seacliff Pines.

Jennifer lingered at the door.

"Nothing's missing," Alex said.

Jennifer, strangely, was not surprised. She walked slowly over to where Alex stood and saw that he was right. Both of Hester's hands were attached to her body. "She certainly looks life-like," said Alex.

"Yes," said Jennifer. For one horrible moment she thought she would cry. "Thanks," she said; although she did not know what she had to thank Alex for.

"I don't think you should..."Alex began.

"Please," she interrupted. "No advice. I know what I saw and let's leave it at that." She turned and went from the room. As she stepped into the corridor, she heard the creak of a door hinge and glancing swiftly to the left saw Miss Dee's door close very softly.

Sleeping pills! She thought scornfully. Had Leila Dee cut off Hester's hand, placed it in Jennifer's bed while she slept, then sewed it back on the body as she talked with Miss Collingwood and Alex downstairs? She hadn't inspected the hands too closely; she didn't want to. But surely Alex would have noticed. But he wouldn't say anything, if they were in it together, if they were both scheming to frighten her from the house.

John returned unexpectedly the next day, ringing the bell around noon while Jennifer was having a belated breakfast. She was so delighted to find him on the doorstep, she flung her arms around his neck, kissing him over and over again.

"So you missed me," he laughed.

"Yes, yes, I did."

"So did I. I sold everything and decided to leave the show early. Like to go for a ride?"

"I'd rather walk. Okay?"

"Fine. Better get a sweater. It's a little chilly."

They went through the woods to the edge of the cliff where they could look down at the small scimitar shaped, sandy beach below.

John, seating himself on a grassy ledge, drew Jennifer down beside him. "How has it been?" he asked.

"Terrible," she said. She told him about the hand and about her suspicions. She had to tell someone; there was too much inside her. When she had finished, John remained silent, gazing out at the water. She wondered what was he thinking. Did he believe that her story of the hand was silly or imagined. Maybe it was.

The sea glittered, a hard blue-white under the noon-day sun. A faint smudge on the far horizon became a long, low ship, plumed with smoke, steaming southward.

"Jennifer," said John, finally turning to her. "You're living under the same roof with a couple of lunatics. It doesn't sound safe."

"Oh," she said carelessly. "I can take care of myself." As always, the sun, the bright day and John's company minimized her danger, shrunk her fears.

"You might be sticking your neck out for very little in return."

"I don't understand."

"I hate to say this, but now that I've had a good look at Seacliff Pines, I've come to the conclusion that it's a white elephant."

"But you said...what about the couple from

Iowa? The ones who were going to be wild about the house?"

"It's a slim chance, Jennifer. Not worth risking your peace of mind for. Well—sensibly now, the house *is* ugly. There are some Victorian places, I'll admit, which have a certain charm, that carry a feeling of nostalgia, but Seacliff Pines..."

"Dismal?"

"Right. All that heavy dark wood, stained glass and faded velvet. Even without the two bodies, it's depressing."

"You never said that before."

"No. I didn't want to discourage you. But it doesn't even have a view of the sea, except from the attic."

She picked a foxtail from the cuff of her slacks. "Then what do you think I ought to do?"

He took her hand, covering it with his own. "Leave. Let the others squabble over it."

"Leave?" She thought of Miss Collingwood silently flitting through the downstairs rooms, dusting and cleaning in the library where Hubert sat. She thought of Leila, her ripe figure draped in pink satin, waving her ivory cigarette holder possessively over the art objects. But mostly, she thought of Alex, his sarcastic grin, the way his eyes rested on her with self satisfied, smug look.

"No," she heard herself saying, "no, I can't give him—them," she corrected herself hurriedly, "...the satisfaction."

"But you may be hurt. You don't know how fanatic gold-greedy people can get..."

"They're trying to scare me, is all. I don't think any of them would dare risk harming me." But was she sure? There was Hester's mysterious death and the flat tire, and Mr. Peters gone, and the

153

statuette crashing down near her head. But she deliberately pushed those thoughts aside. With John as her ally she felt strong, safe.

"Be reasonable," John persisted. "You're scared."

"Who said I was scared?" she asked, and smiled. "Well, Okay, maybe a little. But I'm not anymore. I'm staying," she added stubbornly.

He sighed. "I'd feel a whole lot better if you wouldn't.

He put his arm around her. "I'd never forgive myself if anything happened to you." His face was very close. He was going to kiss her, and she felt curiously detached. She noticed for the first time a scar on his left cheek, a white scar partially hidden by his sideburns. She wondered how he had come by it.

"You mean a great deal to me, you know," John said.

His kiss was ardent enough, but she found herself unable to respond. Was she afraid of falling in love with John? He was the sort of man it would be nice to be in love with, peaceful, secure. There would never be any question of his smiling and winking that would spread charm over a large section of the female population. He was one of the few men left, she argued with herself, for whom monogomy was probably a way of life. Why then was she hanging back? She felt that that certain chemistry was missing.

John pulled her to her feet, drawing her into his arms. He kissed her cheeks, her hair, her throat. She thought again how unmoved she was by his passion, how calm, and wondered if he could ever rouse her and set the wild blood running through her veins the way Alex had done by a mere touch.

CHAPTER XII

"Does Seacliff Pines mean so much to you?" John asked softly.

They had returned to the house and were sitting on the steps of the veranda where stray wafers of sunlight moved in changing patterns on the brown, weathered boards.

"I suppose it is foolish—but, yes," Jennifer replied. "I *counted* on it. I gave up my job—no loss that, and I suppose I could get another. And I sunk all my money into coming out here. I had all kinds of dreams about traveling." She spread her hands.

"You could always join me in potting and real estate." He drew her close. "I could use a partner.

"Me?"

"You. Give up the whole mess and marry me."

"Are you serious?"

"Never more." He leaned over and kissed her lightly on the mouth.

"I...I'm kind of overwhelmed," she hedged. "Do you want an answer right away?"

"Not at the moment, no. But give it some serious thought. I'm going to San Francisco again in two weeks. We could be married there."

"Two weeks...! You don't even know if I can cook," she laughed.

"All right. Cook me a dinner, then. Not here, though, at my place."

"Okay, I will, tomorrow night?"

"It's a deal." He kissed her again and left, driving off with a wave of his hand.

Jennifer, reluctant to go inside, was still sitting on the steps when she was joined by Alex. He had come out the front door, settling down beside her, and she wondered if he had been observing her and John from the entry hall.

"I wanted to talk to you," he said after a moment.

"About what?" She raised her head to watch a bird fly off.

"About the price of rice in China, the weather, sealing wax, cabbages, anything. Just to talk." A pause. "It gets mighty lonely here."

"Why don't you talk to Leila Dee or to Miss Collingwood if you're that hard up?" she asked.

"Leila Dee's trying to seduce me, and Miss Collingwood doesn't talk."

"You could always leave, you know," she said. "You don't have to stay at Seacliff Pines and be bored."

"Oh—I didn't say I was bored. I said lonesome." He was wearing a deep blue sweater, and it brought out the blue of his eyes. She never realized how alive, how expressive blue eyes could be.

"*I'm* not lonesome," she said.

"No, you have the scout master."

"The what?"

"Your boyfriend, the scout master." He grinned.

She thought of getting to her feet and leaving him with a curt word, a scornful look. But that would be running away, an act of cowardice, and she knew intuitively that he would be quick to recognize it as such.

"I've been revising Hubert's memoirs," Alex said, after a few moments of silence.

"Is that what you wanted to talk to me about?"

"I thought it might be an interesting topic. Aren't you the least bit curious about your great uncle?" He seemed genuinely puzzled.

"I...I never knew him. I suppose I am."

"He and our erstwhile burlesque queen, Leila Dee, had a flaming affair until Hester came along and broke it up."

"Was that Leila's version? She told me that she introduced Hubert to Hester, but didn't say anything about an affair."

"Of course, she wouldn't say anything. After all, according to Leila, she's getting the house because Hester was such a dear friend. And nothing could be further from the truth."

"Is that what Hester told you?"

"Hester never mentioned Leila Dee. She didn't want people to know she was in burlesque. But there's a letter I found, a letter Leila wrote Hester thirty-five years ago. In it she threatens to kill Hester if she doesn't stop seeing Hubert."

"So Hester couldn't have left Seacliff Pines to Leila, unless she was the kind who forgave and forgot."

"Not Hester Kirkwood. She carried grudges."

Through the olive green branches of an eucalyptus, Jennifer noticed the sky was beginning to turn pearl gray, the harbinger of fog. She asked, "And what else did you find?" It was out before she had realized it.

He stared at her for a long moment, and she forced herself to meet his eyes without flinching. "Nothing much of interest," he said.

"I'd like to read that book of memoirs," Jennifer said.

"I still have some work to do on it." He stretched his legs out and studied the tips of his shoes.

"*Is* there a book?"

He grinned. "Of course, there is."

The wind stirred in the trees, whirling dried leaves along the gravel drive, ruffling Alex's hair. He did not seem at all like a con man, a disreputable character trying to cheat Hester Kirkwood's great-niece out of her legacy.

"You're staring again," Alex accused, his blue eyes were smiling.

"I was just wondering..."

"Wondering what?"

"If...if you *are* Hubert's grandson."

"Funny," he said, "I was just wondering about you. How do I know you're Hester's great-niece?"

"You can call Mr. Emmett in Chicago if you have any doubts," she said coldly.

"I already have," he said easily. "He gave me a rather hazy description: brown hair, lovely brown eyes, pretty face, beautiful legs. A description like that could fit half a dozen girls."

She got to her feet. "I don't see why I have to justify or prove my identity to you, Mr. Donaldson!"

She was at the door when he called. "Jenny? How's about having dinner at the Lodge with me tonight?"

"No, thank you!"

Someone was walking in the upper floors of the house. Jennifer lay on the pillow listening, her eyes wide in the darkness. Creak, creak, the soft footsteps seemed to drag across the ceiling, creak, creak, creak. Then there was silence. She waited while the seconds thrummed by. Her ears and heart were straining to hear.

The sea, a quarter of a mile away in high tide, boomed in muffled monotony. She pictured it during a flood, obliterating the crescent shaped beach, rolling in, wave after wave, against the cliff. The fog she could picture too, thick and moist, pressing a gray, hungry face against the windows behind the heavy brocade curtains.

Those footsteps again! They were fainter now. It was Alex, she was sure, Alex prowling about, shoeless, flashlight in hand. If there were papers or letters he wanted, then why didn't he conduct his search in the daylight? Why wait until they had all gone to bed?

The arrogance of the man stung her again. More than that she was angry with herself for stalling, for not confronting Alex openly. She got out of bed, drew on her robe, belting it tightly. Earlier she had come upon a flashlight in one of the kitchen drawers and had brought it up to her room. The batteries were weak, and she had meant to replace them but had forgotten to pick some up at the store. Nevertheless, the weak-beamed flashlight was better than groping her way through the dark. She took it, unlocking the door and going out into the passageway.

After her experience in the attic Jennifer had been hesitant to venture beyond the second floor again. But now in her chagrin she forgot her fear. The thought of Alex padding around in stockinged feet, congratulating himself, banished everything but the need to catch him by surprise—red handed.

The nightlight at the head of the stairs, gave enough illumination to guide her down the corridor. She passed Leila Dee's room, and at the bottom of the staircase opposite the room Alex had claimed as his "half" of the house, she switched on the flashlight. Guided by its feeble beam she began to climb the stairs. She moved cautiously, but the floor boards protested loudly under her slippered feet, and she cringed at every step. She paused when she got to the third-floor landing. From where she stood she could look down the stairwell and see a portion of the corridor below. She thought she heard a faint sound coming from behind one of the doors and instinctively doused her light.

Suddenly a door opened and Alex stood framed in a dim amber light. His hair was touseled, and his tanned torso was bare above pajama bottoms.

Jennifer's hand froze to the bannister, her heart thumping painfully in her chest. Had he been in his room all along? Or had he returned a minute before she had come out into the corridor?

Alex yawned and looked up to the top of the staircase. It seemed to Jennifer that his eyes had found her; though she knew she was standing in complete darkness. Alex scratched his head, yawned again, shrugged and closed the door. He had given every appearance of a man roused unexpectedly from sleep.

Had he been pretending? Jennifer wanted to believe that he had, for if he had not, who then had she heard pacing to and fro in the midnight hours across the floor above her ceiling? But even as she pondered the question, her ears caught the whispered, rusty complaint of a door opening behind her. The sound ran like an electric current through her body, lifting her hair on end. Was it Miss Collingwood or Leila Dee?

Her hand tightened on the bannister. Was the ghost of Hester wandering through the rooms of Seacliff Pines? Was her invisible step creaking the floor boards, her phantom hand inching doors open and banging them shut?

Unable to bear the suspense, Jennifer wheeled about. A dark shadow stood very still a few yards from her. Her throat tightened. She could hear the door wheezing on its hinges as it closed slowly. The shadow did not move. Her terror grew. She wanted to turn and run back down the stairs. She did not want to stand there pinned, nailed to her hypnotic fear; she did not want to think of ghosts or half-buried bodies, or of Hester's ghost taking over Seacliff Pines after dark. But she was too terrified to turn her back on the shadow that was facing her now. She feared that *thing,* motionless, watching her with hidden eyes.

She stood there for endless moments, her feet rooted to the carpet, her clammy hand welded to the bannister. Suddenly a funny, little throat-clearing sound came from the shadow. Almost instinctively, she raised the flashlight and pressed the button.

A bearded face hung in the yellowed light beam, a lined face with steel-rimmed spectacles behind which pale blue eyes blinked at her. Below the face the dim light revealed a short man with bowed legs.

"Mr. Peters?" Jennifer heard herself half-exclaim, half-question.

The little man turned and began to hurry away.

"Wait...! Mr. Peters, please wait..." Jennifer urged as she followed.

But she could hear him ahead of her, moving in a peculiar limping, running walk. There was another staircase at the other end of the corridor, one Jennifer had been unaware of until now, and the little man disappeared down it.

"You needn't be afraid," Jennifer called as she went after him.

Midway in descent the flashlight gave out, and Jennifer hesitated for a few precious moments in the blackness. Then, slowly, blindly, she felt her way down to the bottom, and opening a door, she was surprised to find herself in the kitchen. Apparently the staircase, like those in many old Victorian houses, had been designed for the servant's use.

The click of the screen door caught her ear. She hurried across the kitchen to it, and opening the door, came face to face with the thick, wet fog. "Mr. Peters!" she called. She wanted to talk to him. There was so much he could explain. "Mr. Peters!" She heard running footsteps fading into silence.

She stood listening to the sound of dripping moisture, falling drop by drop from the sodden leaves, while in the distance the tidal sea surged and ebbed.

Both Leila Dee and Miss Collingwood said they had heard Jennifer calling during the night. Miss Collingwood had assumed Jennifer was in the midst of a nightmare; and Leila had thought "that awful dog" had returned, and Jennifer had been chasing it through the house.

"Then you must have heard footsteps too," Jennifer said to Leila Dee, who had made no mention of sleeping pills.

"Oh, I always hear footsteps," she said nonchalantly.

It was one of Leila's rare appearances in the kitchen, and she, Miss Collingwood and Jennifer were sitting in the breakfast nook having late afternoon coffee.

"Always?" Jennifer asked. "Here at Seacliff Pines, you mean."

"Yes, here. But old houses do that," Leila said, helping herself to cream and sugar.

Jennifer watched as she spooned three heaping teaspoons into her cup and then began to slowly stir it with one ringed finger daintily extended.

"Those footsteps last night belonged to a little man called Mr. Peters," Jennifer said.

Miss Collingwood blanched. "Mr. Peters!"

"Who's he?" Leila Dee wanted to know.

"The taxidermist who did the Kirkwoods," Jennifer replied.

"What a zany thing to do," Leila said. "Scared poor Charlie out of his head. I'll have to move them. Donate the pair to a museum. Although, I just might keep Hubert."

"You don't really want the house to live in, do you?" Jennifer asked Leila.

"Not the way it is. I'll do a little re-modeling. Put a bar in the parlor, paint the walls..."

Miss Collingwood looked shocked. "The paneling...?"

"Sure. Who wants all that dark wood? I'll do the parlor and the library in creamy white or bright yellow. Yes, I like the place." She patted the plastic tablecloth with plump hands. "I'm not afraid of it the way you are, Miss Collingwood." She shook her finger playfully at the housekeeper. "Scaredy cat."

Perhaps Leila Dee wasn't afraid. Perhaps she couldn't feel the malevolence in the house the way Miss Collingwood and Jennifer could. Or perhaps she was one of those rare people who had never known the meaning of fear. But that was to be proved wrong. Miss Leila Dee was no more immune to terror than either the housekeeper, or Jennifer. And the former burlesque queen showed it in a dramatic way that very night.

Jennifer had been asleep for several hours when she was brought awake by the sound of a woman's scream. Her sleep-drugged brain failed to place where the shriek had come from until it echoed again through the house. It was a terrible sound which sent her heart thumping. It had come from one of the bedrooms along the hall.

Trembling, Jennifer got out of bed and searched blindly for her robe. In the meantime silence had settled in, more terrible than the scream, a silence which was like a black calm imbued with the substance of appalling finality. She found the robe and with cold, shaking fingers drew it on.

Glancing irresolutely down the corridor, Jennifer saw a band of light across the carpet in front of Leila Dee's room. She hurried toward it and pushed her door open.

Leila's stout figure lay sprawled face up on the floor. Her rouged cheeks were two flaming spots on a chalk white face. Alex stood over her. He had a poker in his hand.

CHAPTER XIII

Their eyes met across the room and held. Jennifer felt her cheeks go red as wave after wave of emotion passed through her; shock, disgust, fear. "What have you done?" she asked, when she managed to find her voice at last.

"Me?" Then glancing down at the poker, as if he were seeing it for the first time: "Now, look here, Jenny, it's not what you think. I heard her scream and I thought...." He took a step forward, and she shrank back.

"Don't come near me," she warned.

"Oh for God's sake!" Alex threw the poker aside and getting down on his knees beside Leila began to chafe her wrists.

"Make yourself useful." He turned his head to Jennifer who had remained standing at the door. "Pour me a glass of wine." With his chin he indicated wine bottles on the bureau.

"You didn't..." Jennifer began, not trusting him yet.

"Hit her? No."

"What happened?"

"Beats me." His voice was edged with irritation. "When I got here she had already fainted."

Leila began to moan. Jennifer moved quickly, then, to the bureau and finding a half-full bottle among the litter of empty ones. She filled a glass with wine and brought it to Alex who lifted Leila's head and put the glass to her lips. Leila's false eyelashes fluttered and her eyes opened. "Drink," Alex commanded.

Leila's throat muscles moved as she swallowed, her eyes rolling from side to side.

"Do you think you can stand?" Alex asked.

She closed her eyes for a moment as if in pain, then nodded in the affirmative. Alex helped her up and over to the bed. Leila, groaning, sank down heavily.

"Will you tell this lady here," Alex said, indicating Jennifer, "that I didn't bash you over the head."

"No," said Leila. "No. I almost wish you had, instead..." She looked up at Jennifer. "I never believed..." She swallowed, her eyes widening. "It was *her*."

"Who?" asked Jennifer, knowing the answer but asking anyway while a cold shudder worked itself down her spine. "Who?"

"*Her*. Hester!"

Alex made an impatient clucking sound in the back of his throat, and picking up the poker said, "If you'll excuse me, ladies...?"

"No, Alex, wait, I want you to hear..." Leila protested.

"Tomorrow," he said smiling and left.

"He doesn't believe me." Leila shuddered. "Do I seem like the hysterical type to you?"

"No," said Jennifer.

"May I have another glass of wine, dearie?" Jennifer filled the glass again. She noticed how Leila's hand shook as she brought it to her lips. "I saw her. And...oh, my God...!" She drank. "...I

166

don't think I'll ever forget it. She came at me with a kitchen knife."

"A ghost with a kitchen knife?" Jennifer could not help the incredulity in her voice. She had a sudden picture of Miss Collingwood in the pantry. "Are you sure it was...it was Mrs. Kirkwood you saw?"

"I swear it. I'll swear it on a stack of *Bibles* if you want me to."

"You weren't sleeping?" Miss Collingwood could have come into the room wearing a dress belonging to her dead mistress, carrying the same carving knife which had frightened Jennifer. In the dark it might be hard to tell them apart since they were both short women.

"I wasn't asleep," Leila Dee said firmly. "I was wide awake. I was sitting on the lounge doing my nails."

Could Miss Collingwood have masqueraded as Hester's ghost and come up to the second floor and scare Leila Dee half to death?

"She didn't say anything. She just stood at the door, glaring at me," Leila said. "Then she started toward me—that's when I fainted."

Suppose Miss Collingwood's timidity, her fear of Hester's ghost, was all pretense, a put on, a cover for her own maneuvering to drive the unwanted tenants from Seacliff Pines.

"Why should Hester take a knife to you?" Jennifer asked. "I thought you two were bosom pals."

Leila stared at Jennifer for a few moments. Her mascara had smudged, emphasizing the pouches under her eyes. "She hated me," she confessed. "You see, Hubert was in love with me, not her.

But..." She stopped suddenly, her eyes going wide with fear again.

"But what?" Jennifer asked sharply, bringing Miss Dee to attention.

"But nothing," she answered, just as sharply, "I'm packing. You'll have to help me. I'm packing and leaving." She pushed herself to her feet.

"Now? It's three o'clock in the morning."

"Now, now, *now!*" She went to the closet and brought out a large suitcase and threw it on the bed.

"There's no one to take you. You can't call a cab..."

"You'll drive me," she said authoritatively. She moved to the bureau and opened a drawer, scooping its contents into her arms.

"Not me," said Jennifer. "The fog is as thick as pea soup."

"I'll get someone," said Leila. "I'm not staying in this damned haunted house a minute longer than I have to."

"I thought..."

Leila turned on her. "I don't care what you thought. I don't want to ever see or hear of Seacliff Pines again. It's a dump—a dump! Charlie was right. Now, hand me those shoes on the floor."

She turned back to her packing, her hands tremulously folding lingerie, and Jennifer realized that despite her brusque voice, Leila was still very much frightened.

"That letter..." Jennifer began.

"You can have it—you can have the damned house. I'll sign it over to you now." She got her handbag and rummaged through it. "A pen, do you have a pen? Never mind, I've found one." She took another sip of wine. Then grasping the pen, pursing her lips, she spoke as she wrote: "To who it may concern. I, Leila Dee, leave the house to Jennifer—what's your last name, dearie?—Sargent. Jennifer Sargent. No strings attached. Leila Dee." She thrust the paper at Jennifer. "Now it's yours. All of it."

Jennifer wanted to ask if the letter shown to her when Leila had first arrived had actually come from Hester, but she saw no point to it now.

It was a sleepy, disgruntled Alex who was finally pressed into driving Leila Dee into Carmel. She left in a flurry, muttering that the house was cursed and that Hester had always been a spiteful bitch with a flair for stirring up trouble.

The next morning Alex claimed that Leila Dee's vision of a vengeful ghost was the result of too much wine. "Drank like a fish," he said.

But Jennifer wondered. She wished she could get inside Alex's head and know what he was *really* thinking, what he was planning. It didn't seem logical that a man gainfully employed (even a free-lance writer) should hang about Seacliff Pines waiting for a lawyer's decision, unless he was there for another purpose.

And there was Leila Dee, someone Jennifer had thought was as hard as nails, fainting, actually fainting because she believed she saw a ghost. Jennifer was aware that Leila drank, but she did not think she had been *that* inebriated.

There was something very strange and frightening going on within the walls of Seacliff Pines. It was a drama which seemed to be rolling inexorably toward some horrible denouement. Jennifer could not help but sense danger; it was in the very air she breathed.

Then why did she stay on? Why didn't she take

John's advice and leave? Stubborness and unwillingness to be pushed around could go so far and then it became stupid bravado. She didn't necessarily have to abdicate, as John had pointed out. She could take a room at the Lodge or find a cheap motel until Mr. Emmett made up his mind. She sat and debated with herself, arguing pros and cons and finally came to a decision. She would give Mr. Emmett two more days. If he had not determined Alex's status by then, she would leave Seacliff Pines—at least temporarily.

Toward evening a fine rain began to fall. Jennifer had completely forgotten her promise to cook dinner for John until the doorbell rang at six. He looked very solemn when she opened the door. Before she could speak, he said, "Jennifer, I'm really sorry, but I'm going to beg off on our date." He came into the hall, drops of rain clinging to his jacket and his hair. "A client is coming down from San Francisco. He wants to discuss a couple of houses I've shown him."

"That's all right," Jennifer said. "We can make it another time. Can you stay a minute?"

He glanced at his watch. "No—I don't think so." He put his arm around her waist. "Damn it, I was looking forward to this evening."

"Why don't I come over in the morning," Jennifer offered, "and fix your breakfast?"

"Would you? I'd love it." He kissed her.

The smell of the sea and wet earth wafted in on Jennifer as she closed the glass doors on John's departure. She could hear the rain drumming on the roof of the veranda and gurgling in the rain gutters. Shivering in the damp, stale chill which pervaded the house, she switched off the hall light and went down the passage to the kitchen.

Miss Collingwood was sitting at the table and staring moodily into a coffee cup. The stark, overhead light gave her face a saffron tinge and brought out the wrinkles in her forehead, making her look old.

"Shall I get us something to eat?" Jennifer asked cheerfully.

Miss Collingwood continued staring.

Jennifer repeated her question and when she received no answer, shrugged and began to prepare her own meal, salad with hard boiled eggs, lettuce, tomatoes and cottage cheese. She was at the sink washing the lettuce leaves when Miss Collingwood suddenly spoke.

"What?" asked Jennifer turning the water off. "I didn't hear you."

"She walks every night now," Miss Collingwood said, turning glazed eyes on Jennifer.

No amateur actress could be that good, Jennifer thought again; no untrained person could portray fear so well.

"But she hasn't shown her face to me yet," Miss Collingwood went on. "One day she will." A shudder went through her body, and she put her head in her hands.

"You mustn't say such things," Jennifer admonished. "You're talking yourself into a state."

"I'm afraid," came Miss Collingwood's muffled voice. "I'm afraid." Then to Jennifer's consternation she began to cry. "I can't bear it," she sobbed.

Jennifer went over and put her arm around the housekeeper's frail shoulders. Jennifer felt helpless and guilty. "I told you I would try to get you another job." She hadn't, of course, made a single attempt, a single inquiry. How could she when the house was not legally hers yet?

"There's no one who cares." Miss Collingwood sniffed and wiping her nose on a paper napkin, she said "No one ever cared, except Hubert." She lifted a tear-stained face to Jennifer. "He loved me, and she killed him because of it."

Jennifer's arm dropped away from her shoulders. "What are you saying?"

"She did it with a kitchen knife, a big carving knife, and then she had Mr. Peters sew him up."

Jennifer felt sick.

"I should have killed *her* myself. I should have done it years ago." Twisting the paper napkin in her hands, she fell silent.

"Did you?" Jennifer's voice cut the stillness. "Did you kill her?"

Miss Collingwood said nothing. Her large eyes looked beyond Jennifer to some distant vision.

Jennifer went back to the sink. Miss Collingwood rattled her cup and said, in a surprised tone, "What are you doing?"

"Washing lettuce. I'm going to fix a salad."

"I've already had my supper," she said. Rising to her feet, she carried her cup to the sink. "When Miss Dee left did she say anything about the money she owed me?"

"Why no," Jennifer said amazed. Miss Collingwood could change from talk of murder and ghosts to practical matters in the blink of an eyelash. God, she was weird. "Maybe she'll mail it to you."

"I doubt she will," Miss Collingwood said with the resigned air of one who had given up on positive expectations. "Well, goodnight then."

Listening to the rain, Jennifer ate her salad. She could barely hear the surf; perhaps the tide was out. The clock on the shelf jerked the minutes one by one past the hour. She was wondering if Alex had gone out when, suddenly, a horrible crash and the sound of a heavy object bumping down stairs broke the silence. There was a final thump against the door—the door which led to the servant's staircase. And then silence.

Jennifer sat at the table, her fork poised in mid-air.

A fresh burst of rain splattered against the windows. Jennifer put the fork down. A choked groan came to her through the door. It sounded like a deep moan of pain.

"Who is it?" she called. She got up, shaking the table, her fork rattling in the dish. "Who is it?"

No answer. Not even a groan.

She went to the door and listened, fearful, hesitant. She slowly twisted the door knob. The door would only open halfway. Something was jammed against it. She stuck her head through and saw Alex lying on his stomach. His eyes were closed, and his face was a ghastly white under his tan.

CHAPTER XIV

Squeezing through the door, she stepped over Alex's prone body and knelt by his side. One lock of hair had fallen over his forehead, and with a tentative, uncertain hand she brushed it aside. She revealed a lump the size of a goose egg. Already it had turned a sickly purple at the edges. His eyelashes, darker than his hair, made two sooty crescents under his closed eyes. His arms were thrust out above his head, his hands half clenched. He looked so defenseless, so vulnerable; he might have been any young man innocently asleep in his bed.

She touched the bruise gingerly with a finger and 'Alex's eyes flickered open. He stared at her dully, uncomprehendingly, then closed his eyes again.

She took one of his hands in hers. It was a cold hand, and she began to chafe it. His hand was large, well shaped; the nails square cut and clean. After a few moments she glanced up suddenly and caught his open eye watching her a split second before he shut it again.

She leaned back on her heels. "All right, Alex, you needn't pretend." Taken in again, she thought angrily; she was the great humanitarian.

Slowly, groaning loudly, Alex turned over on his back. "Why did you do that?" he asked, addressing the ceiling.

"Do what?"

"Push me." He blinked his eyes at her, then put his hand to his face. "Phew...!" shaking his head, "...dizzy!"

He wasn't faking; she realized that. He couldn't pretend, not with that bump on his head. "What do you mean, 'push you'?"

He removed his hands from his face and studied her. In the diffused light his eyes were a shadowed, deep blue. "Didn't you push me down the stairs? I want an honest answer, Jennifer."

Jennifer, instead of 'Jenny.' He *was* serious. "No," she said, meeting his gaze steadily. "How could I? I was in the kitchen eating my supper when I heard you fall."

He kept staring at her.

"Why should I push you down the stairs?" she asked, getting to her feet.

"Hoping I might break my neck, maybe?"

"If that were the case," she said, looking down at him, "I wouldn't have tried to revive you; would I? Are you sure you were pushed."

"I may have big feet, but I'm not the kind to fall over them." He took hold of the stair post and pulled himself up.

"It wasn't me."

He brushed the hair back from his eyes. Even with the ugly bruise on his forehead, he looked unbelievably handsome. "If it wasn't you, Jennifer, that leaves three possibilities."

"Three?"

"Miss Collingwood, Hester or Hubert."

A feathery current of cold air seemed to brush the back of her neck. "Miss Collingwood never goes upstairs. And if you're trying to scare me with ghost stories, it won't work."

"I'm not trying to scare you," he said slowly. His

175

voice had changed pitch. He was looking at her in a different way, too. His eyes were saying things, sending all kinds of erotic messages.

"I . . . I have to go . . ." she gestured toward the kitchen. The space at the bottom of the stairs, flanked by doors, was small and close. He was inches from her, but he made no move to touch her; yet she was held by his magnetism just as surely as if she had been pinned in his embrace.

"Do you always run away?" he asked softly.

"No . . ." A lie, she knew it and wondered if he did too, but the rack and thumb screw could not wring the truth from her, not here, not now. She ran from John because she did not want to commit herself; because, she rationalized, she did not feel she loved him. She was not afraid of John. She could handle him. Alex she could not.

"How can I thank you for trying to help me?" he asked, and smiled.

"It was nothing," she said, wrenching her eyes from him and pulling the door open.

She walked slowly across the kitchen to the breakfast nook, her ears alert for the sound of his footstep behind her. But none came. A moment later she heard him ascending the back stairs.

It was eight forty-five when she finished tidying up, putting away the last cup, wiping the stove for the third time. When she finally closed the kitchen door behind her, she had the sudden sensation that she had left a haven of safety and stepped into a dark and hostile world. The passage was icy cold and the heavy, paneled walls seemed to lean toward her, narrowing the way. Why should the house seem so changed, so different from the kitchen? It's because the kitchen was warm, she

176

answered her question, and the rest of the house was unheated, drafty and cold.

But she knew in her heart it was not the difference in temperature which made her so anxious. Perhaps it was Alex's fall which weighed on her mind. Had he tripped accidentally, then accused her of pushing him, simply to tease or to bait her? Or worse, had he deliberately thrown himself down that staircase to divert suspicion from himself? He might have reasoned that it would be difficult to cast as a villain a man with a purple bump on his forehead.

She wondered where he was at the moment. In his room? Or stealing silently along the corridors upstairs? If only she had some miraculous device, some clever periscope, whereby she could keep track of his movements.

She hurried along the dark passageway to the foot of the stairs and pressed the switch on the wall. The light on the landing came on. It was a luminous, soft spotlight that enhanced the shadows beyond. In little flowing curls of damp cold, eddying about her ankles, the rain driven night seeped under and through the double, glass doors.

She looked up at the length of the staircase with a sudden innate repugnance to climb it. It was all so foolish, she told herself. What was she afraid of? She could not understand why she had this fear when she had traveled the kitchen passageway, had gone up and down those stairs so many times in daylight and in dark. Why did she fear tonight, especially? Foolish. She couldn't give in to every little trickle of doubt, every scarey whim. She would be a mental case, like Miss Collingwood, in no time, if she did.

Grasping the bannister, she began to climb. She was midway up when the light at the top suddenly went out and darkness dropped over her like a smothering black curtain. Jennifer clutched at the rail, and the fear which she had managed to rationalize away, came back in an overwhelming tide.

The lights have failed, she told herself. A weak bulb has died. But her senses informed her otherwise. Someone was there; someone was at the top of the stairs.

"Alex...?" Jennifer's voice trembled in the dark. "Alex...?"

A breathless whisper reached her ears, a whisper so slight she could not be sure she had heard it at all.

"Alex..." She bit her lip. "Alex, please don't play games."

Down below her the rain beat a faint tatting sound on the veranda. Far away the sea heaved and sighed, and sighed again.

"Alex...turn on the light."

She heard a quick intake of breath, as if he were suppressing mirth. It was Alex; she knew it was him.

Still she waited, her hand on the rail. Should she go back down the stairs or continue upward? It was safer to go back, she decided.

She turned and then with the realization that she was probably visible, if even faintly, because of the opaque, gray light from the glass doors, she shifted to the wall side of the stairs.

A sound above, a sharp cracking, brought her to a halt. Later she was to wonder what mysterious inner voice had warned her, but, at that moment, suddenly, instinctively, she flattened herself against the wall. Just as her cheek touched the smooth paneling, the staircase shook and a heavy object came hurtling down. It jolted and bumped past her. A half-second later there was a loud splintering crash as the object reached the floor below.

Jennifer's knees trembled; her sweating hands slid along the wall; and she had a moment of dizziness when she felt as if she were going to fall, tumbling after whatever had barely missed her. Slowly, like someone affected with palsy, she lowered herself and sat down on the step and put her head between her knees.

The night light went on. Alex's voice exclaimed, "What on earth...?"

She lifted her head and turned. Alex, his forehead plastered with bandages, came quickly down to her. "What happened? Are you all right?"

She didn't answer. He stretched out his hand to help her up, but she shrank away. "I swear..." he began and then whistled.

She followed his gaze and saw the great stone urn, the same one with the drooping peacock feather she had noted that first night. It was lying in green, jagged pieces on the floor of the hall. The urn had been moved from its place beneath the fanlight and shoved down the stairs straight at her.

Slitting her eyes against the light, she looked up at Alex.

"For God's sake, Jennifer. You don't think I did it?"

Digging her nails into the carpet, she turned away.

Alex made an exasperated sound in the back of his throat. "I didn't touch that urn any more than you pushed me down the back stairs. Don't you see what's going on?"

She looked up at him again. Half in dark shadow his face looked grim, but then he met her eyes, and a small sympathetic smile began to show. He couldn't be a murderer, she thought; could he?

She took his offered hand, and he pulled her to her feet. "Someone," he said, guiding her up the stairs, "doesn't like us."

"Who?" She tried not to lean on him, but her legs felt shaky.

"Miss Collingwood. Oh, I know she doesn't ever come up the stairs. That's what she claims anyway. But can we be sure? I mean, she could sneak up and down the back staircase four times a day without either of us being aware of it."

"That's true. But I can't imagine her having the strength to move a stone urn." She shuddered as she recalled the thundering crash.

"Weak people, especially those with loose screws like our Miss Collingwood, usually have iron wills strong enough to move mountains. Don't let her scared eyes fool you."

They had arrived at Jennifer's door. "What shall we do?" she asked Alex. She wanted very much to believe it was Miss Collingwood who was responsible for all the mysterious and terrifying events at Seacliff Pines. How much simpler it would be to really know it was an unbalanced housekeeper than to wonder about Alex or to keep edging around the uncomfortable question of an occult manifestation.

"I'll ask her," Alex said.

"You don't expect Miss Collingwood to confess?"

"No. But she'll know we're suspicious, and she might be afraid to try anything again."

"She seems so genuinely frightened, timid..." Jennifer mused, remembering Miss Collingwood's tears in the kitchen.

"She's not frightened of me, and I don't think she is of you, either."

"You're really convinced it was her, aren't you?"

"Have you got any other suggestion?"

Yes, she wanted to say. It could be him. She had grave doubts about him. She didn't know whether he was speaking the truth or not. "No," she said. "I can't think of any at the moment."

"Well, then, in the meantime, if I were you, I'd lock my door."

"Oh, I will." She turned and opened it.

"Jennifer..."

He had moved. He was right behind her, his body just barely brushing hers. "If you're afraid of spending the night alone...."

"I'm not," she said, and she went in quickly, shut the door and twisted the key in the lock.

When she awoke the next morning, her first feeling was one of relief; she was still in one piece, still in full possession of her faculties, still alive. The house hadn't triumphed yet. Then she remembered she had promised to cook breakfast for John, and she was glad for something to look forward to, something to do. It was eight o'clock; she had plenty of time. She got up and dressed.

Mentally ticking off the breakfast menu—pancakes, eggs, sausages, coffee—she wondered how well stocked John kept his kitchen. But she had all the makings downstairs.

Fifteen minutes later she was in the pantry packing a shopping bag. She hurried, hoping not to meet up with Miss Collingwood. She wondered what had transpired between the housekeeper and Alex after she had gone to bed, and she felt a little sheepish because she had allowed Alex to blame Miss Collingwood for the falling urn (among other things) without coming more strongly to the housekeeper's defense. They had no proof of her guilt, and she remembered how upset Miss Collingwood could get when wrongly accused.

A light rain was falling when she turned into John's driveway. As she approached the house, she saw through the moving windshield wipers that his car was gone. A little annoyed and disappointed, she parked and went up the wooden stairs. The door was locked, and there was no note tacked to it as she might have expected if he had been suddenly called away. From her pen in the back yard, Rena began to bark.

Jennifer waited another half-hour. Because the place, with its vacant air, reminded her of Mr. Peter's brooding house, she started the car and left. She decided to go into Torrey, do a few errands, call Mr. Emmett, and perhaps by the time she got through, John would have returned.

It was ten-fifteen when she put her call through to Chicago. To her surprise Mr. Emmett himself answered the phone. "Oh, yes, Miss Sargent," his voice came to her on thin threads of sound. "The Kirkwood estate. Just a moment." She heard paper crackling and then Mr. Emmett clearing his throat. "Ah...here it is. Well, Miss Dee's letter from Hester Kirkwood seems authentic. It's Hester's handwriting, all right. But I don't think..."

"Miss Dee is gone," Jennifer interrupted. "She doesn't want the house."

"Oh?" Mr. Emmett's voice registered surprise. "When I talked to her, she sounded so positive."

"She claims she saw Aunt Hester's ghost," Jennifer said.

"My, my," Mr. Emmett clucked. "She didn't seem at all like a fanciful woman, but then one never knows...never knows."

Jennifer was tempted to tell him that perhaps Miss Dee wasn't all that fanciful, that there were all sorts of weird things going on at the Pines, but she knew that the old lawyer would cluck at her too. How could she possibly convey through the impersonal medium of the phone, the feeling of Seacliff Pines. How could she give even a hint of its brooding malevolence?

Jennifer said, "Do you know how or of what Mrs. Kirkwood died?" That, she felt, she could ask. It was a concrete, sensible question.

"Heart failure, I believe it was," came the answer. "The death certificate said heart failure."

"Who was her doctor?"

"I can't recall at the moment. Why do you ask?"

She hesitated. No, she couldn't tell him of her suspicions, not without some tangible proof. "Just curious," she said.

"I'll look it up and let you know, if you wish. But there's something else..." A silence. "...yes, here it is. There is an Alexander Kirkwood. His father,

Oscar Kirkwood, was Hubert's son by a first marriage. However, I think it is rather peculiar that the young man, claiming to be the grandson, has done so through the mail with me rather than in person. He'll have to make an appearance here, I'm afraid. We'll need his fingerprints, among other things."

Of course, Mr. Emmett was right. "I'll give him the message," Jennifer said and hung up. The questions, the nagging worry and the suspicions were still there. Nothing had really changed; nothing was really settled. Though Mr. Emmett had proved the existence of someone called Alexander Kirkwood, the identity of the handsome blond man at the Pines was still in doubt.

She had given herself two days. Now she must wait until Alex himself went to Chicago. Would he go? Or would he linger for another week or a month and then disappear altogether?

As she left the phone and was threading her way through the narrow aisles of the store, she passed the post card rack and suddenly remembered that she hadn't sent a word back to the girls at Goodbody's. They had given her a farewell lunch and bought her a gift—a small camera—and she had promised to write.

Her eye ran over the selection of post cards: an orange sun setting gaudily through fringed palm trees, the blue Pacific stitched in white, the waves caught in frozen perpetuity, the leafy aisles of tall, lofty redwoods. She chose one of the latter.

The post office, partitioned off from the general store by a thin, wooden wall, could be reached through an inside door with a high threshold. She went across it to the little ink-stained wooden shelf which held two old fashioned inkwells and a bentnibbed pen. She took her own ball point pen from her purse and began to write, "Dear Gals..."

What could she say? Certainly not the truth. In any case it would take volumes to explain. She gazed out the side window at the cars whisking by with a wet, rubbery sound, then bent her head and began to write again. "The weather's a bit rainy, but the scenery is lovely..."

"Pardon me, Miss."

It was the postmaster with several handbills. "New batch just arrived," he said, thumb tacking them to the board above the wooden shelf, under the lettered notice, "MEN WANTED BY THE FEDERAL BUREAU OF INVESTIGATION."

"Popular gents," the postmaster quipped. "Some ladies too."

Jennifer looked down at her card. She had taken care of the weather and the scenery; what else could she say? She lifted her head. She was thinking, studying absently the bills on the board. Suddenly her eyes focused. She leaned upward. She saw the face—so familiar—a face she had seen so often in the last few weeks. If you took away the beard...

Robbery, fraud, theft and forgery.

No, it couldn't be. Her heart started to pound in her ears.

Age: thirty, five feet, ten inches, brown hair; sometimes poses as blond. Alias: Jed Murphy, Jack McIntyre.

No, her imagination was working overtime again. But the shape of the eyes was the same; the color too. And the nose, and the scar; there was a white scar on the right side of the face. John McGraw.

CHAPTER XV

"But it can't be!" Jennifer repeated aloud, and standing next to her licking and pasting stamps, an elderly woman with a white cloud of hair, said, "I beg your pardon?"

"Oh..." said Jennifer, smiling weakly, "nothing. I was just talking to myself."

The woman smiled in return and patting the last stamp in place, left to deposit her mail in the slot.

Alone, Jennifer's eyes went back to the stark, black and white photographs. *It can't be,* she thought silently. Fraud? Robbery? Of all the people in the world John was the last she would call a criminal. He was a decent man, a man who wanted to share his life with her, wanted to marry her. She trusted him.

It was just a resemblance, that was it, an uncanny resemblance. Yes, it *had* to be. People were always being mistaken for someone else. When she saw John she would tell him he was headlined at the local P.O. She'd make an amusing story of the episode, and they would both have a good laugh.

But—suppose, just suppose it *was* him. Suppose John McGraw and Jed Murphy, alias Jack McIntyre, were the same person. She had to admit that except for the one time when he had told her

he had come to Torrey ten months earlier from
Missouri, he never spoke much of his past. He
never mentioned details of his family, friends, or
business associates.

But did that make him a criminal?

Yet there were other things, little things, which
nagged at her; his frequent absences, for instance.
He was always taking off for San Francisco. Craft
shows, he said, where he could sell his ceramics.
But from what she had seen at the cottage, his
output of pitchers, cups and bowls was meager,
and even to her unprofessional eye they were
rather amateurish. And what houses had he been
showing to prospective clients? Now that she
thought of it, he had never actually described any
of them.

Then there was the matter of his not having a
phone. She knew that business phones had first
priority, and after ten months it would seem that
John, supposedly a licensed realtor, would have
one installed by now. Was he reluctant to apply for
a telephone because he might have to answer
questions, give references, make himself known?

It also occurred to her that John had never
taken her to a public place for a meal or even a
drink. The meals they had together were always at
his house or at Seacliff Pines. In the past she had
imagined his reluctance to invite her to the Lodge
or to a restaurant in Carmel was due to his lack of
money, but now she wondered. Was he afraid of
being seen? She recalled, too, that whenever he
drove her to the general store, he had always
elected to remain in the car while she shopped.

But lastly, and most importantly, there was that
scar, that white, puckered scar partially hidden by

his sideburns. Could two people have identical scars?

Looking out through the rain-streaked window, Jennifer felt as if an unpleasant, staggering burden had suddenly been thrust onto her shoulders. What should she do, call the highway patrol, the sheriff? There were many expensive summer houses hidden among the folds of the coastal cliffs, one of which John might be in the process of burglarizing at this very moment. This man in the picture *did* defraud, *did* steal, and she knew that if he had robbed her—Jennifer Sargent—of anything, she would feel justly indignant. After all hadn't she gone on and on about Alex and Leila Dee, and how they were trying to cheat her of Seacliff Pines?

She put the postcard in her purse and snapped it shut. She looked at the MAN WANTED bill again. It seemed that the resemblance between the photograph and John was not quite as marked as it had been at first sight. Was she jumping to all sorts of ridiculous conclusions?

She would talk to John, she decided; it was the only fair thing to do. She would bring the subject up obliquely, see how he reacts, and play it by ear. There was no point in going off half-cocked to the police without giving John a chance to speak for himself.

But when she reached John's house, he hadn't returned yet. She scribbled a hurried note, "Please come over. Missed you for breakfast." She slid the note under the door where he would be sure to find it.

The rain had stopped by the time she arrived at

Seacliff Pines. Looking up, she could see a rift in the smoke gray clouds. That scrap of blue sky cheered her. Perhaps she worried too much, worried needlessly. John, Alex, Miss Collingwood and the whole mess, somehow, would work itself out.

As if to affirm her decision to lay worry aside, the sun poured through the now widened gap in the clouds, and for a few brief minutes as Jennifer refastened the garage doors, the wet, dripping world was lit with a dazzling, crystaline light.

She went back to Seacliff by the way of the brick walk which led to the back entrance of the house. Rounding the corner, she jerked to a halt. A man lay sprawled across the walk, his head hidden by an overhanging fuchsia. Horrified, she squatted on her heels and pushed the moisture laden bush aside.

It was Mr. Peters!

His eyes were closed; his face was a waxy white. His eyeglasses, unbroken, were clutched in one hand. "Mr. Peters..." Jennifer whispered, lifting his hand and feeling for a pulse. He wasn't dead, but he looked it, even more so than Alex had when she had found him at the bottom of the stairs.

She ran into the house. Alex, sitting at the table, his eyes glued to a book propped up against the sugar bowl, was absently dunking a doughnut in a glass of milk.

"Come quickly," Jennifer said breathlessly. "It's Mr. Peters...he's outside...on the walk."

Alex got to his feet at once and went out through the screen door. Jennifer followed. Kneeling, Alex studied the still face, felt the old man's pulse, as

189

Jennifer had done. "I'm no doctor," he said, "but seems like the old man has had a stroke. Do you see where one side of his face has gone all funny?"

"Yes," Jennifer said, feeling cold, helpless and depressed. The sun had gone in again. It seemed that nothing joyful, even a happy mood temporarily brought on by sun between rain clouds, could last at Seacliff Pines. "Is there a doctor fairly close we can call?" she asked.

Alex touched the old man's face with the tip of a finger. "I think the best and quickest thing to do is to take him up to a doctor in Carmel."

"But is it wise... what I mean is... should you move him?"

"What else is there to do? We can't leave him here."

He lifted the little man in his arms. His salt and pepper hair-covered head sagged like a rag doll's. "Run on ahead and get the garage doors open, will you?"

She did as he asked, thinking that the one good thing about Alex was his quick, calm reaction in an emergency.

"I'll have to take your car. Mine hasn't got a back seat," he said as he walked toward the garage.

"Of course," she said, opening the car door for him. Alex laid the old man gently down. "Do you want me to come with you?" Jennifer asked, giving him the keys.

"No, it won't be necessary." He removed his jacket and pillowed it under Mr. Peter's head. "I wonder what he was doing here?" he muttered.

"You know him?" Jennifer asked.

"I met him several times when he came to see

Hester. They were old friends. I've tried to look him up, but couldn't seem ever to catch him at home.

"He...I saw him one night—here."

Alex gave her a sharp look. "You did?"

"Upstairs on the third floor. When I called to him, he ran."

"Oh? Why do you suppose he'd do that?" Alex's eyes were watching her closely.

"I don't know," she said, "unless..."

"Unless what?"

"Unless he felt guilty about something."

Alex studied her for a moment longer. "I guess I'd better be on my way," he said. Jennifer stepped aside as he shut the back door and got in behind the wheel. "Oh, by the way," he said, looking up at her. "I haven't had a chance to speak to Miss Collingwood. I'll do that when I get back."

He started the car. "Are you sure you don't want me to come along?" Jennifer asked again, her uneasiness for the old man growing.

"I can manage," he said, his voice edged with annoyance.

"I hope he's all right," Jennifer said and found she was talking to herself as the car slid out into the drive.

She watched them jolting and splashing through flooded potholes until the car disappeared around the side of the house. Alex had not wanted her to come along. Why? After weeks of trying to get close to her, to become "friends," as he put it, inviting her time and again to have dinner at the Lodge, he had suddenly rejected her company. Was he afraid Mr. Peters might regain consciousness and say something damaging? And how odd, she mused, going into the kitchen, that Mr. Peters had had his attack only a few feet from the kitchen window where Alex had been sitting, dunking doughnuts, seemingly unaware.

Odder yet was Mr. Peters' presence at Seacliff Pines. Where had he come from and why? This was the second time she had encountered him on the premises. Was he looking for money or had he returned for some other purpose like blackmail, for instance? He could be blackmailing Miss Collingwood or Alex. If it were Alex, she thought, with a sudden catch of her breath, then the old man would never survive the journey and reach a doctor alive.

Sitting in the parlor where she had a good view of the bottom of the drive, Jennifer anxiously waited for Alex's return. There was a book in her lap, but she had long ago given up the pretense of reading. The grandfather clock in the entry hall cleared its throat and struck the hour. Bong— bong—bong. Three o'clock. Alex had been gone a little less than two hours. She figured she had about another hour to wait. The last hour dragged and when Jennifer finally heard the car through the trees, she ran out to meet it. Alex waved her down to the garage. She reached him there as he was closing the garage door.

"How is he?" she asked anxiously.

"Didn't make it," he said, looking grim.

"He died then." Though she had prepared herself for the worst, she was shocked.

"He was dead before I got to Carmel."

She bit her lip. She felt terrible. She hadn't known Mr. Peters; he might have even been a murderer, but she felt terrible, nevertheless. "Nobody will ever find out," she said aloud. Mr. Peters had kept his secrets.

"Find out what?" Alex's tone was sharp.

She hesitated a moment. "Nothing."

Had Alex made sure of Mr. Peter's permanent silence? It would have been easy for him to reach back and cover Mr. Peter's small bearded face with one of those big hands and snuff out the barely lingering breath.

They walked toward the house without speaking. "Oh," said Jennifer suddenly. "I almost forgot. I spoke to Mr. Emmett, and he told me you're okay."

"That's nice to know."

"He says, however, you'll have to appear personally to be fingerprinted."

Alex looked at her questioningly.

"Well—he has to make sure."

"I suppose so. You aren't sure either, are you?"

"I…" She kept her eyes straight ahead. "No."

"I'm glad you said no." He was smiling. "It's one of the few straight answers you've given me."

"Are you suggesting I'm devious."

"Yes."

She felt too depressed to argue.

They had reached the back door. Alex paused and looked up at the sky. "Rain again."

Through a leafy arch of trees Jennifer saw a scowling mass of purple clouds, their underbellies reddened by the dying sun. Until that moment she had not noticed the hush, the quiet, heavy torpidity of a lull before a storm, which had descended upon the world. The charcoal tree trunks, the jade branched bushes, a discarded, dented watering can, everything she looked at was delineated in unreal metallic light.

She felt a sudden inexplicable pang. What was she doing here, she wondered as she stepped through the door into the dim kitchen? Why had she come? Why did she stay?

In the distance she heard the first, far off grumble of thunder, and it ran through her like a shudder.

"We don't usually have thunderstorms on the coast," Alex was saying. "But this looks like a big one."

She was hoping John would arrive before the storm broke. She wanted desperately for him to come; she was sure in her mind, now, that he could not possibly be a criminal. She longed for someone she could trust, someone to remove the burden of doubt and fear from her shoulders. Every passing hour, every passing day seemed to pull her deeper and deeper into dread. And John had offered to take her away, away from this bleak, cold house. Why hadn't she listened to him?

"I'm going upstairs," Alex said. "I'm bushed."

She almost asked him to stay (in spite of her mistrust of him) so acute was her feeling of loneliness. Even Miss Collingwood's silent, sullen company would have helped.

The sky outside grew darker; the thunder growled, skulking around the chimney tops of Seacliff Pines. John should have returned home and read her note by now, she thought. But why didn't he come in answer to it?

The kitchen curtains billowed in a draft as blue-white lightning glimmered behind them.

She couldn't wait for John. She would go to him. It was ridiculous, utter foolishness to sit alone in the house with this feeling of impending disaster when she didn't have to.

She ran upstairs, grabbed her hooded raincoat and changed her shoes for boots. The white lightning shimmered along the dark paneled walls as she came down again. She opened the glass double doors, and a bolt of electric blue danced crazily across the veranda. Thunder crashed with a deafening clang of iron striking iron, and the sky yawned open. Rain lashed, and a sudden high wind swept her into a vortex of whirling fury. She clung to the door jamb as the blinding light came again, and after it followed peal after peal of thunder.

Pulling herself inward, she shoved the doors shut against the raging elements. It was impossible to go out. She would hardly be able to negotiate the driveway, let alone the winding, rain sheeted road to John's house. She would wait; perhaps in an hour or so it would storm itself out.

But the rain and the wind increased, steaming the windows in battering gusts of fury; the thunder once dying, came to crashing life again. And above the sound of the driving rain, Jennifer could hear the sullen roar of the sea—so close it seemed as if the waves had climbed the cliff and were, with each succeeding booming surge, coming closer and closer to the house.

Jennifer went to bed early. Propping the pillows up behind her and setting a book on her knees, she soon found that she was reading and re-reading the same sentence while her ears listened. The house was like a ship, battling a tempest at sea.

Creaking and groaning, shivering and shaking with each new onslaught of wind, the house was hammered relentlessly by driving gusts of rain.

At ten o'clock the lights flickered and went out. Jennifer, in the darkness, thought she heard the distant crash and tinkle of broken glass. She was unsure where the sound had come from, upstairs or down below. She had visions of billowing, brocaded draperies, the wet rain beating on the carpet, or perhaps on one of the velvet chairs in the parlor. "There's nothing I can do about it," she rationalized.

But she knew her reluctance to investigate sprang from sheer cowardice. Beyond the safety of her room there was chaos, the unknown, and she did not have the courage to venture out into the blackness of the corridor.

She must have fallen asleep shortly afterwards. When she awoke in the morning, she found that electric service had been restored. Her bedside lamp was tinging the gray, drab, early light with a sick, yellow glow.

The room was ice cold, and she dressed hurriedly, throwing a sweater around her shoulders before she went downstairs to the parlor. None of the windows there, she saw, had been broken. And a subsequent check of windows and lamps on the ground floor failed to find anything amiss. Perhaps she had imagined that sound.

The wind had abated, but the rain was still coming down in a steady, unremitting downpour. The trees stood tall, their drenched branches wrapped in misted shrouds. The water at the foot of the drive ran in deep rivulets ending in a small pond beyond the veranda steps. She wondered again if John had come home. She supposed he had. There was Rena to be fed. Perhaps, she hoped, he would drive over after lunch.

Noon came and went. She had a quick meal and sat in the parlor with the same book she had tried to read so many times before. She hadn't seen or heard Alex. Miss Collingwood in her wraith-like fashion had, without a word, slipped in and out of the kitchen. Three people under the same roof, Jennifer mused, and each of them might as well have been marooned on their own separate island.

A half-hour went by. Hearing footsteps on the veranda, Jennifer's pulse quickened. It was John, at last. She ran to the door only to find it wasn't John, but Alex. He entered, stamping his feet, shaking the water from his blond head. "The drive's still passable," he said. "But I don't know what it's going to be like if this keeps up."

"Oh, I hope we're not flooded!" Jennifer exclaimed with feeling.

"Would it be that bad?" Alex asked.

"Yes," she said and went back to the parlor and her book. If John didn't show up by three, she promised herself, she would drive over to his place no matter how hard it was raining. Thinking something may have happened to him, she was beginning to worry.

At two-thirty the rain had slowed, becoming a fine drizzle. Unable to bear the tension of waiting any longer, she got into her raincoat and went out. Wading through the small pool at the bottom of the veranda steps, she went around the house. When the stone terrace came into view, she saw what looked like a dark heap in front of the French doors. She drew closer and her heart skipped and then began to thump loudly in her ears. The heap was a man, John McGraw.

He was lying face down in a dark pool of rain and shattered glass. She did not need to touch him to know that he was dead.

CHAPTER XVI

Jennifer began to swoon; the scene blurred and focused, blurred and focused, swinging in and out like a lamp in a storm. To steady herself, she leaned forward over the balustrade, and for a moment she felt that she would be sick. But, as a breeze stirred the trees above, spattering a shower of raindrops on her covered head, the dizziness passed. The mist, pungent with eucalyptus, lay against her cheek like a cold, wet hand.

She forced herself to look at John. Shrunken and pitifully lonely, his body seemed oddly small under the sodden, slate colored sky. The pool of water about his half-crushed head was dark with blood. John. Somehow it was difficult to connect that prone, outflung figure with the John who had held her hand, kissed her and asked her to marry him. A tear blurred her vision and trickled down her cheek. Was it possible she had harbored all those unkind thoughts and had even wanted to call the sheriff because she had believed him a criminal?

She gripped the balustrade, trying to steady herself, trying to think. She did not have to be a doctor to realize that John's death had been caused by a powerful blow on the head. Apparently, John had come to see her, had been waylaid and killed. And there was only one person at Seacliff Pines who had the muscle to crack a man's skull—Alex.

Alex must have killed John McGraw; probably before he had come stamping into the house at one o'clock, shaking the rain from his shoulders, saying the drive was passable. He hadn't gone out to check on the condition of the drive. She saw that now; he had slipped out earlier in the rain to wait for John and to kill him.

Why?

She did not flatter herself to think Alex had murdered John out of jealousy. She knew Alex was attracted to her, but he was not insane enough to kill a man because of it. No. The only possible motive she could come up with was that John, in some way, had posed a threat to Alex.

She began to shake again, her knees knocking together. She had to get to a phone. She had to call the sheriff before Alex became aware of her absence.

The sudden rattle of the French doors startled her, and looking across the terrace, she saw Miss Collingwood standing behind them. Her white face was pressed against the glass, her hand at her throat. A moment later Alex appeared. He opened the doors and stepping out knelt quickly at John's side. "My God!"

Go! A voice within Jennifer urged. *Go*! But weakness overcame her, and she could not move.

"He's dead," Alex said, and Jennifer thought what a consumate fraud the man was. He was always ready with the appropriate tone of voice, the make-believe shock, the dismay.

"Does John's death surprise you, then?" she heard herself say as she glared at him with hate filled eyes.

He twisted his head and stared at her across the rain-drenched terrace. "Are you trying to say *I* killed him? What a damn fool!" he exclaimed, getting to his feet. "Why? Why should I have murdered John McGraw? And if I had, do you think I would have left him lying here on the terrace for all the world to see when there are five acres of brush and trees and, God knows, how many gullies to hide him in?"

There was logic in what he said, and it shook her a little. Had she come to another hasty conclusion?

Alex glanced down at John's body, and then he leaned back. Looking up, he said, "He must have fallen from there," he said, pointing to the turreted attic.

Jennifer, following his gaze, saw that one of the tall narrow windows in the attic had a gaping black hole. She stared at it for a half-minute, her mind blank, and then suddenly she recalled the sound of shattering glass she had heard during the storm. Confusion and bewilderment whirled in her mind. What did it mean? Why had John fallen from an attic window? The house rose above her in its implacable, ugly and secretive way. *It* knew. She had never hated Seacliff Pines more.

"I'll have to call the sheriff," Alex said.

"Yes," she nodded, parting reluctantly with the last shred of suspicion. Alex wouldn't summon the law if he was guilty.

"Can't we bring him inside?" she asked.

"No. We'll have to leave him here. We don't know for sure whether it was an accident, suicide or murder. Miss Collingwood would you get a blanket, please?"

The sky had grown black with clouds, and a few drops of rain began to fall on the terrace.

"By the way," Alex said to Jennifer, "did you know John was in the house?"

"No, I didn't. I had no idea."

"He didn't come to see you last night?" His eyes were sharp and probing.

"No," she said. "I haven't seen him since and day before yesterday."

Miss Collingwood brought the blanket, and Alex covered John's body.

"I heard the window break last night," Alex said. "But I thought it was the storm. Funny isn't it, that he should go through a closed window like that? I'm going to run up and have a look before I leave. Want to come?" Jennifer hesitated. "Still don't trust me, do you?" He said with a smile.

Was she acting foolishly? "Yes, of course, I trust you."

Together they went in and started to climb the staircase. "Were you aware that John McGraw was wanted by the FBI?" Alex asked.

Loyalty to John held her tongue for a few moments and then she said, "I saw a picture in the post office that looked like him, but I didn't think..."

"That John McGraw and Jed Murphy were the same?"

"Yes," she said in a small, barely audible voice.

"Well, they are—or were."

They continued in silence until they reached the narrow turret staircase. "How can you be sure?" Jennifer asked.

"I saw that picture of him, too, and like you I thought it was just some guy who resembled John. But the other morning when I was in the general store, I happened to look through the post office door and there was John acting very peculiarly. His eyes were nervously looking all around without his head moving. Then suddenly he reached up, tore something from the wall and stuffed it into his pocket. Later I went in to see what he had taken. His picture was gone. Now, you know he didn't take it home for a wall hanging. He was scared somebody would see it and recognize him."

Jennifer, reaching the top step, paused to catch her breath. "Why didn't you call the sheriff, then?" she asked.

"What and have you say I did it out of spite? I thought you were nuts about the guy."

She looked away without speaking.

"There's another thing," Alex went on. "I found him trying the doors, one night, up on the third floor. When he saw me, he very coolly said he was just looking the house over because he had promised to sell it for you."

"When was that?"

"Last Tuesday, I think."

That was the night John had come over to tell her he had the appointment with the man from San Francisco. And, of course, long ago he had told her the house was a white elephant, that it couldn't be sold.

They went into the attic, windy and wet with rain. There was shattered glass, old clothes, books and empty cigar boxes which had spilled from the opened drawers of a bureau onto the floor.

"He was looking for something," Alex said, pointing to a flashlight on the floor. Jennifer recognized it as John's. "Looking for Hester's money, I bet."

Jennifer's eyes went from the open drawers to the flashlight. She felt sick. Discovering that John had been a felon had shocked and disappointed her, but to find that he had lied and used her to gain entrance to the house, was repellent. She recalled when the dog had come scratching at the door on the night John was supposed to be at a craft show and how restless Rena had been, how she had howled and barked at the closed doors. Was it John's scent she had caught? Had he been at Seacliff Pines that night? John had been her friend, kind, helpful, someone she had leaned on in her distress. Had he loved her at all? Or had every word he had said been a lie? He was dead now, and she would never know.

She stared at the rain falling in straight, gray lines past the gap in the window. She set her jaws against the threatening tears.

"Are you all right?" she heard Alex ask.

Not trusting her voice, she nodded in the affirmative.

Alex held the door open for her, and they went out of the attic and silently down the stairs.

She had been fond of John. And perhaps in time she might have even come to love him. But now she only felt hurt and bewildered. For it was John all along, she realized, who had been trying to frighten her and the others from the house. It was he who had attacked her in the attic, sent the stone urn hurtling down upon her and thrown the statue from the window. He must have come and gone secretly from Seacliff Pines time and again. He must have walked the half-mile from his house along the beach and used the crude shell and stone staircase on the side of the cliff; the staircase he had claimed was unsafe. He was a burglar, the notice had read, and burglars were adept at managing locked doors and windows with noise-less ease. Perhaps he had been searching for Hester's money even before Jennifer had met him, the day he had stopped the car and asked pleasantly, "Could I give you a lift?"

Her throat swelled with the memory.

"I have an apology to make," said Alex. They had reached the entry hall and were walking back to the kitchen.

"What's that?" Jennifer asked.

"I didn't really think it was Miss Collingwood who scared Leila Dee away and pushed me down the stairs. I thought it was you."

Astonished, she looked at him. "I thought *you* were the one who...who was trying to get rid of *me*."

They both laughed a little nervously.

"Well, now we know," said Alex. "Are we friends?" There was that intense look in his eyes again.

She gave him a thin smile. "I suppose." She should be grateful to him for not gloating over John's deception, for not scolding or chiding her because she had mistrusted him. But she couldn't shift her feelings from active dislike to warm acceptance that quickly. Perhaps that would come later.

"If you're afraid of staying here and want to come along..."

"No," she said. "I'll be all right. I don't think I should leave Miss Collingwood alone."

"I'll make it as speedy as I can," he said, before he let himself out the kitchen door.

The sky had grown darker, the inky, shadowed trees tossing their heads in the rising wind.

Jennifer put the kettle on and brought the jar of instant coffee from the pantry. In the distance she heard the explosive pop-pop of Alex's car as he gunned the motor going past the house. The rain dashed against the windows in sporadic fits. She thought of John's body lying alone under the sodden blanket. How had he fallen from the window? A miscalculated backward step? "Why don't you leave?" he had urged her. He hadn't wanted to hurt her. He had only wanted her out of the way.

The kettle began to whistle. She turned it off, thinking that Miss Collingwood might like a cup of coffee too. She went down the passageway to the housekeeper's room and rapped at the door. After a moment, Miss Collingwood's faint voice called, "Yes?"

"Care to join me for some coffee?"

"Thank you. I'll be along in a little while."

Back in the kitchen Jennifer sat drinking black coffee, nibbling on a graham cracker, when a sudden clap of thunder startled her out of her reverie. Another electrical storm? She hoped not, but as a precaution she went to the pantry and brought out the candles, a miscellany of stubs and clotted tapers, the same ones Miss Collingwood had used when the lights had failed some weeks earlier. She looked for fresh candles but found only one which she stuck in a tarnished brass holder. Beside it she set a box of matches.

Glancing up at the clock, she saw that it was only a quarter-to-six. Alex had been gone almost an hour, but it seemed more like three. She wished she had something to do, someone to talk to so that time wouldn't drag. She thought of Miss Collingwood again. Perhaps the housekeeper hadn't wanted her company, or perhaps she had fallen asleep.

Jennifer twitched aside a curtain. The trees, the shrubbery and the walk were starkly lit by the momentary lightning. Thunder growled, bumping along overhead in sullen reverberations. Jennifer pulled down the shade on the windows and locked the back door. She did not want to admit to a growing uneasiness. Why should she be anxious when the cause of anxiety—John McGraw—was no longer there?

Clicking on lights, she went through the dark paneled passage. When she came to the front door, she locked and bolted it. With her face pressed against the thick glass of the door, she watched lightning shimmer and throb, illuminating the needled rain against a background of wind-twisted foliage.

The hall light dimmed and wavered, went out and came on. Jennifer scurried back to the kitchen. Striking a match, she began lighting all the candles and setting the smallest ones in saucers. Her hands were trembling so violently that she dropped a candle and barely rescued it before it rolled off the counter.

"This won't do," she told herself. "I'll be a gibbering idiot by the time Alex gets back." She bit her underlip and forced her hand to steadiness as she put a flame to the last candle. Then she poured herself another cup of coffee and sat down at the table. Lightning crackled, and she ducked, involuntarily wincing. She wasn't afraid. What was there to be afraid of? This wasn't the first thunderstorm she had encountered. But her body refused to be calmed; every muscle was tense, waiting and listening.

Suddenly, above the sound of the rain, she heard the slap-slap of a window shade somewhere on the lower floor of the house. A window had been left open in one of the rooms, she realized with a cold shudder. Had it been open all this time?

Slap-slap. Was it coming from the direction of the dining room? She went to the kitchen door and peered out. Slap-slap. It was the dining room. Yes, of course, she thought and brightened; the French doors which led out to the terrace were in the dining room. Earlier when they had come in after covering John, they must have neglected to close them properly.

She took a lighted candle—just in case—and walking down the corridor, came to the dining room. When she opened the door a cross-current of cold, wet air blew the candle out. For several long, nervous moments she fumbled for the light switch. She found it, and the cut-glass chandelier over-head blazed with sudden light. She saw that she had guessed correctly; the French doors had blown open. Crossing the room quickly, she shut and fastened them. While trying not to think of the blanket covered body just outside, she checked the other windows and doors and turned off the light. Leaving the dining room, she started to make the rounds of the first floor to see if any other windows had been left unlocked. She tried to tell herself that she was taking precautions against the rain coming in and ruining the carpets. But she knew this belated concern for carpets was self deception. She felt unsafe and threatened. The house, the dark night and the storm frightened her.

She left the library to the last. She thought of skipping it altogether. The vision of Hubert's presence, sitting in eternal silence behind that closed door, raised goose pimples along her arms. But, calling herself an idiotic coward, she went in anyway. She made herself walk past Hubert's glassy stare, and going to the windows she began to inspect the locks on each one. She had finished the last one. Satisfied that the room was secure, she turned to leave; when suddenly, without any warning, the lights blinked out, and she was plunged into utter darkness with a dead candle in her hand. For a minute everything was black panic. She wanted to scream, to run. It was as if she had been buried alive in a dank grave with a moldering corpse, and she felt herself on the verge of disintegrating into chattering madness.

But somehow, like a shipwrecked sailor clinging to a bobbing spar, her mind held to a sliver of reason, and with her heart beating wildly in her throat, she began to feel her way across the black void toward the door. She had taken only a few steps when she stumbled. Crying out in terror as she grasped something hard and sinewy, she thought for a horrible, nauseating moment it was Hubert's hand, but her fingers recognized it as the claw of a stuffed parrot which sat on one of the tables.

She reached the door at last. Crossing the threshold into the corridor and before she could take a deep breath of relief, she heard pattering footsteps overhead and the slamming of a door. Her heart began to thud anew. All around her the darkness and the black shadowy doors of the corridor seemed to leer at her; the carved, angel faces convulsed in satanic amusement. Beyond the glass thunder spat, and light throbbed, throwing everything into eerie relief.

"It's Miss Collingwood," she told herself, "those footsteps are Miss Collingwood's. She's gone upstairs for something."

But Miss Collingwood never went upstairs.

Jennifer ignored the thought and closed the library door behind her with damp, clammy hands. Groping her way back along the passage, she came to the kitchen where the candles gleamed and danced, throwing misshapen silhouettes against the papered wall. She took the tall candle in the tarnished brass holder and went out again. With her shadow following along the dark wood of the narrow passage, she arrived at Miss Collingwood's door.

Jennifer knocked again and again with firm, insistent knuckles. "Miss Collingwood?" Silence answered her.

An unshaded window at the end of the corridor blazed for a split second as lightning flashed, and thunder spilled, booming from the sky. The house trembled and shook.

Growing more and more uneasy, Jennifer turned the doorknob. Holding the candle high, she saw the bed, the smooth bedspread, and the undisturbed bolster. She swung the light around past the bureau, the closet and the wide open door of the bathroom. It was a neat room, sparse, tidy, like Miss Collingwood. But it was empty of her presence.

Then she *had* gone upstairs. But why? What would draw her up there in this frightening storm? Perhaps the housekeeper was not afraid anymore. Perhaps she had reasoned that it was John

McGraw who had been impersonating Hester Kirkwood's ghost, and there was no longer any reason for her to avoid the upper stories of the house.

Jennifer retraced her steps to the back staircase. "Miss Collingwood?" she called up into the hovering emptiness. The house echoed her voice as if mocking it. Then with her shadow still beside her, Jennifer walked to the front of the house and repeated her anxious call. Only the sound of the incessant rain, the dull drumming on the veranda and the mutter of dying thunder answered her.

Had something happened to Miss Collingwood, or was her silence deliberate? Jennifer stood in the entry hall listening to the storm without and the tick-tock of the clock within; a cold fear swam through her veins as all her former suspicions of Miss Collingwood returned.

Except for removing her fear of Hester's ghost, John McGraw's death had really changed nothing for Miss Collingwood. She was still a woman who felt she had been grossly cheated and ill rewarded for years of servitude. Could she be blamed for wanting what she thought was her just share of the estate. Perhaps she wanted all of it. Jennifer recalled the wild glint in Miss Collingwood's eyes the day she faced her in the pantry. She thought of the years of suppressed hatred building and building like a boiling volcano in that flat, seemingly timid breast. Hester was dead, and Mr. Peters too; secrets shared among all three of them might never be known.

Could Miss Collingwood get the house by default, Jennifer wondered, if there were no blood heirs to claim it? Probably, she could. And here she was, Jennifer thought, alone in a house, a vast house whose geography still remained vague to her, alone with a woman who is half mad and seething with vengeance.

A board creaked, and she swung around. "Miss Collingwood?" she called sharply. The dark walls leapt and shuddered in the wavering candlelight. Jennifer's eyes strained, trying to penetrate the blackness of the passageway. But no one came, no one spoke. Her anxiety grew. She went to the door, and looking through the side panel, she saw in a flash of lightning that the foot of the drive was completely under water. Even if she could get the car started, it would be difficult maneuvering up through the deep mud and flooded potholes.

Her room, she finally decided, was the best and the safest place to wait for Alex's return. There she could lock herself in. But—supposing Miss Collingwood was already there waiting, hiding in the closet and concealing herself behind a door or a curtain? She felt trapped and scared. She tried to warm herself with the knowledge that Alex would be back with the sheriff. But she did not know how soon, or late, and in the meantime. . . .

A muffled scream brought her from the door. It had come from the floor above. After what seemed a long while, Jennifer heard her own wavering voice, "Miss Collingwood?"

Had the housekeeper become frightened? Was she hurt or in pain? Or was that scream a lure?

Hesitating a few moments longer, Jennifer slowly mounted the stairs. At the door of her room she held the candle at arm's length and examined the corners for an unusual shadow and the curtains for a suspicious bulge. There was a heavy, onyx ashtray on the bureau. She tiptoed over to it and grasped it firmly in her hand. She looked in the bathroom and in the closet. She was fearful and expectant, but no one was there.

The rain beat upon the windows. She felt smothered by its repetitive sound, so much like the thumping of her heart.

She went back to the door and peered down the hall. Should she search for Miss Collingwood? She might be unconscious or in a faint. If something really had happened to her, afterwards—possibly tomorrow in the light of day—Jennifer knew she would feel guilty and foolish. In the end she compromised with herself by cautiously venturing from door to door along the corridor, standing at the open threshold of each room and calling the housekeeper's name.

She got to the very end of the hallway and was starting back, when the candlelight picked out a scrap of crocheted cloth on the floor. It was the kind of hand-worked material Miss Collingwood wore as removable collars and cuffs for the few shapeless dresses of her limited wardrobe. The scrap was half-in and half-out of a closet door, a deep closet where old blankets and musty pillows were usually stored.

Jennifer stopped to pick it up and pulled at the bit of linen to work it loose. The closet door slowly creaked open on its hinges, and to Jennifer's dumb-struck horror, a hand fell forward, a small, fragile, blue veined hand. With the tip of a shaking finger, Jennifer ticked the door open a few more inches.

The candle's bright yellow flame fell upon Miss Collingwood's face frozen in death, the eyes staring out with a look of indescribable horror.

CHAPTER XVII

Numb and cold, Jennifer stared at Miss Collingwood, unable to tear her eyes away. "No," she mumbled, "no. Not another."

A drop of hot wax fell on her hand, stinging her to life. Slowly she released the doorknob. All around her the shadows moved closer. Seacliff Pines had claimed one more victim. It was a house of death; John McGraw sprawled on the terrace; Miss Collingwood here at her feet; and behind that closed door in her bed lay another corpse, mummified as was the one in the library. Only she, Jennifer, remained alive. She was the only living being in this Victorian tomb, this mausoleum.

She dragged herself along the corridor to her room. Still clutching the candle, she fumbled with her free hand through the closet for her raincoat. She couldn't stay. She mustn't. It was suicide to remain here where death stalked the corridors, walked the stairs on silent feet and waited, smiling, smirking in dark, shadowy corners. She didn't care about the rain. She *had* to leave.

She tried slipping into the raincoat while her left hand still held the candle as if that slender lighted taper of wax were her life line, her link to sanity. But she kept missing the sleeve; so she set the candle down on the bureau, and then forcing her uncoordinated limbs to her will, she finally got the coat on. Taking up the candle again, she hurried from the room. The journey to the kitchen was a long one, made through an eternity of anxiety and fear. When she finally reached it, she was surprised to see by the clock on the shelf, that she had been gone less than a half-hour. It seemed ages ago since she had left to look for Miss Collingwood.

All thumbs, she pawed through the drawer for the flashlight, and finding it, she suddenly remembered that its batteries were dead. Leaning her head against the overhead cabinet, she pushed back the hysterical panic threatening to engulf her again. She couldn't go to pieces now. Her survival depended on her ability to think and act.

Did she need a light? Perhaps the occasional flashes of lightning could guide her?

Then she recalled the oil lantern she had used when the lights had failed once before. It was kept on a peg in the pantry, and she took it down now. Her heart came alive with fresh hope as she touched a lighted match to the wick and a soft glow fanned under the dusty glass.

She doused all the candles, save one which she placed in the sink for safety. As she opened the back door the great, dark night burst in upon her in a whirl of rain lashed wind and pulsating light. Thunder crackled, hurling downward in a waterfall of deafening sound. The lamp's glow, so heartening in the safe confines of the pantry, was a feeble pin-prick of light in the raging dark.

Holding the hood of her coat to her head with one hand, the lamp with the other, and gritting her teeth against the wind, Jennifer stepped out boldly. Slowly, painfully, stepping carefully over fallen branches, she started toward the garage. If the car did not start she would just sit in it and wait. The garage would be far less frightening than the house, and besides, it wouldn't be long before Alex returned. He had been gone more than three hours, and precluding an accident, he and the sheriff should arrive at any moment. "*Any moment*," she promised herself. "Any moment," she said, repeating it over and over again.

She sloshed through a wide expanse of rain; the icy water filled her boots and soaked her feet. A glimmer of lightning revealed the garage ahead, just beyond the swaying branches of an overhanging oak. She took a firmer grip on the lantern when a blaze of white-hot lightning held her, blinding her eyes. A second later she heard a sharp cracking sound, then another and another as the ground beneath her feet quivered and shook.

Her eyes flew open. Barely two feet from where she stood a branch of the oak had crashed to the ground and had completely obstructed the door to the garage. A cold tremor ran up from her soaked feet. A few steps, another moment or two, and she would have been lying there amidst the wet leaves, crushed, dying or dead. And the car—her means of escape, her refuge—was impossible to reach now.

"God, what shall I do? How shall I ever have the strength to fight this?" she asked herself in despair. It was as if the house were possessed by some diabolical spirit, a force of evil determined to bar her flight. "What shall I do?" she pleaded aloud, her mind going round and round on a hopeless whirligig.

But again, she pulled her scattered wits together. Now, the only way to leave Seacliff Pines was on foot. She turned, waded through puddles and plodded through muddy heaps of debris. Not caring anymore about her feet, already wet and cold, her toes long since numb and lifeless, she came around to the flooded drive in front of the house. She looked up through the trees where the lightning zig-zagged the sky.

"Lightning never strikes twice in the same place," she told herself, but in her heart she disbelieved it. Nevertheless she started through the water, and she was dismayed to find that it was well over her ankles. Suddenly her right foot twisted as it went down into a hole, and she fell full-length, the lamp bounding from her hand. The water was gritty, choking and shockingly cold. Gasping and coughing, she managed to raise herself to her knees and then shakily to her feet. Her ankle throbbed with pain. The lamp—she couldn't find it. Apparently it had broken and gone out. There was nothing for her to do but reluctantly return to the house.

The candle she had left in the sink was very close to gone. She quickly lighted another. Alarmed to see how all the candles had shrunk, some of them to mere waxy puddles, she wondered how long they would last, even if she were to use them carefully one by one. The thought of being completely in the dark was too unbearable to contemplate.

Then, conscious of her dripping clothes, she started for her room, bringing one of the candles with her. It took an act of moral courage to mount those dark stairs; but she got to the top and after hesitating a moment on the threshold of her room, eyes sharp, ears alert, she went in, closed the door and locked it behind her.

She slipped out of her wet clothes and replaced them with dry socks, woolen pants and a warm jersey. Then she went into the bathroom and washed the mud from her face and hands. In the dimly lit mirror her pallid reflection looked back at her out of deeply shadowed and frightened eyes.

She felt better; though her ankle still throbbed. She sat down on the bed and glanced at her watch. It was still running, the hands at half-past-seven. Where was Alex?

Then, as if in answer to her question, she heard the sound of a door closing below, and footsteps. She unlocked her door, and favoring her ankle, she ran as quickly as she could to the head of the stairs. "Alex...?"

The hall clock ticked away; the rain fell upon the veranda.

Perhaps he had come in by the kitchen door. Jennifer, candle in hand, hurried down to the kitchen. The flame of the candle leaped high with the current of air she brought in with her. The kitchen was empty. She heard the drip-drip of the faucet, the quiet purr of the refrigerator. "Alex?"

Cautiously, crossing the floor, she peered into the darkened pantry. Had she imagined those footsteps? She stood listening, straining her ears above the sound of her own loud heart beat. Yes! There they were again. *Footsteps!* They were upstairs walking, walking in her room? Where?

Footsteps!

She ran to the bottom of the back staircase. "Alex...!" Fear was like a dagger at her throat. "Alex...!"

A door whined, slamming shut, a pistol-crack sound in the night. And then, suddenly, it all came together. She knew. Alex *was* in the house. He had never left it!

All the hours she had been waiting for his return, promising herself that she had only to hang on another half-hour, another fifteen minutes, until her ordeal would be over, all those hours was time spent in false hope. He had lied about going for the sheriff as he had lied about everything else. Somewhere on the muddy, rain soaked drive, well hidden from the house, he had parked his car and doubled back on foot.

He had fooled her once again. Hadn't she warned herself from the first, told herself over and over again that his flashing smile was a front, that he was a smooth talker, a con man? She had never asked him about the envelope in his glove compartment, never demanded an explanation for his nightly prowling through the house on stockinged feet. There hadn't been time, she thought bitterly; he had to rush off for the sheriff.

He wasn't a Kirkwood; his name was Donaldson. He wasn't an heir; he was an imposter.

And that story about John McGraw tearing the hand bill from the wall at the post office, had he invented that too? She didn't know. Had he killed John by pushing him out of the window? Had he murdered Hester and Mr. Peters? Alex had probably discovered that Hester was worth a great deal of money, that she distrusted banks and had hidden her wealth in the house. Perhaps John had been looking for it—and had paid with his life. The same thing must have happened to Miss Collingwood.

Was Alex a murderer?

Odd that even now, even in the midst of her fear and her conviction of Alex's duplicity, she couldn't feel sure. She thought of the time she had found him unconscious at the bottom of the stairs, his face white, his features in repose bearing the aura of vulnerable innocence. "Could the man with such a face kill? Why not?" Her cynicism asked. "Was there anything in the rule book which said murderers had to appear sinister and ugly?"

But she didn't have time to debate or theorize. Alex was in the house, and she was alone with him. There was no one now to wait for, no one who would come to her rescue. No friend, no acquaintance, not even a casual passerby had any reason to turn in at the rusted gates of Seacliff Pines on a rainy night and press the front door bell to say, "Hello, I just dropped by." Seacliff Pines was a house which had long ago set itself apart and aloof.

Suddenly she felt drained, tired and defeated. She had lived with anxiety and fear too long. If she could only sit down at the kitchen table and put her head in her hands, give up, not fight anymore, simply wait placidly for whatever fate Alex had arranged for her.

But she knew she couldn't. The will to survive was too stubborn and gradually her brain began to figure, calculate, maneuver and try to find a way out of her horrible dilemma. The first thing she needed was a weapon. Ineffectual as it might eventually turn out to be, at least it would give her courage. She pawed through several drawers and found a hammer with the feel of heavy substantiality.

Next she blew out the candles and waited until

her eyes had adjusted themselves to blackness. Then she stole silently out along the passageway toward the front door. The flooded drive and the storm were no longer objects of fear to her. She would rather drown in a pothole than remain in the house.

She was a few feet from the door when lightning flickered, and in that brief moment her horrified eyes picked out the dark shadow of a figure silhouetted against it. Panic stricken she turned and limped back to the kitchen, dragging herself across the worn linoleum to the outer door, and dropping the hammer, she tugged desperately at it with sweating hands.

It was locked! Alex must have locked it and pocketed the key while she was upstairs changing her clothes.

Like a hunted animal whose mind has been reduced to a single overpowering need to flee, she instinctively rushed out again towards the servant's staircase. There she paused, and moving cautiously, she mounted the stairs. Feeling her way in the dark, testing each step before she put her weight on it, she reached the landing and waited. Holding her breath, she listened. Then hugging the wall, she sidled along until she reached her room. She closed the door softly and locked it. She pulled the heavy chair over from the window and positioned it solidly under the door knob.

She felt safe for the time being. Beyond that she dared not think. Morning would come; the storm would be over. Perhaps she could bargain with Alex, her life for Seacliff Pines and all within.

The room was cold as ice. She went to the closet

for a jacket, found one in the dark and was slipping it from the hanger when she had the sudden terrible sensation that she was not alone in the room. She stood perfectly still while the blood seemed to congeal in her veins. She saw the reflected glimmer of lightning illuminate the sleeve of a dress and the collar of a coat. Thunder clattered in the distance, and in its dying echo, she was certain she heard a rustling movement.

She whirled around.

A shadow was standing near the door. The uncertain light was too feeble for her to make it out; but the shape was all wrong—it wasn't tall and broad shouldered the way Alex's shadow would be.

"Alex...?"

A beam of bright light stabbed her eyes, pinning her against the closet door, and instinctively she raised her arm over her face and closed her eyes.

"Alex... please...."

She heard it then, a sound which froze her heart—the jangle of bracelets. She opened her eyes and found herself looking into the death-mask face of Hester Kirkwood.

CHAPTER XVIII

Time stopped and hung suspended for an eternity in that first flash of recognition. Then slowly a horror such as Jennifer had never known crept like a furry, little monster through her body, crawling over her skin, raising bumps along it, over her arms and legs, her back, her face, under the hair on her scalp.

Hester Kirkwood's ghost!

This, then, was the hidden presence which had watched her as she took the path through the trees, the phantom which had looked down the stairwell as she climbed the stairs, the apparition which had brushed her face in the dark of the night as she slept.

Hester Kirkwood's ghost. The evil, the malevolent, distilled essence of Seacliff Pines. Here before her, *now*! It had come through the door even as she had locked it, thinking she was safe.

The phantom smiled, red lips parting in the yellow mask, and a laugh emerged, small, cruel, a spine chilling cackle.

Jennifer's heart throbbed agonizingly. She thought—in a minute my heart will burst, and it will all be over. This nightmare will be finished. She longed to lose consciousness, for darkness, for the solace of a blank mind.

Then suddenly the lights went on in a blinding blaze.

The ghost was still there. Jennifer stared and stared. And the ghost stared back out of tawny, red rimmed eyes. A dumpy shape dressed in black. "Is...is it you?" Jennifer asked in a strangled voice.

Hester put the flashlight down. She caressed her bracelets, sweeping them upward and let them fall in a jangle. That gesture, so characteristic of her great-aunt, so unforgettable; that jarring, tinkling sound oddly enough seemed to lessen Jennifer's terror, though not her disbelief. "Is it you?" she repeated.

"I've come back from the dead," said Hester in a voice meant to be sepulchral.

Jennifer gazed at the woman, no more a ghost than she was. Puzzled, bewildered, not knowing what to say, Jennifer muttered, "I...I don't understand...."

A long, heavy sigh. "You don't think I'm a ghost?"

"No...not now," said Jennifer. "But who...whose body is in your bed?"

"It's a dummy."

"A dummy?"

Hester cackled. "Looks like me, doesn't it? Spittin' image. Whitlock Peters did a fine job."

She must have been hiding in my room when I came up, Jennifer thought. "Why...why...?" she asked, and the "why's" echoed in her mind. "Why did you pretend you were dead?"

"I wanted to see what would happen," she said. "So I made up that will with instructions to advertise and sent it to Mr. Emmett. I wondered how many claimants would crawl out of the woodwork. How many fools would go searching for money I was supposed to have hidden in the house. Ha! As if I would leave money around. It's all tucked away in a bank, several banks." She jingled her bracelets. "Well, it was just as I predicted. All the vultures came to roost at Seacliff Pines. Leila Dee, wanting to remodel—to *paint* the paneling..."

The very walls had ears, Jennifer remembered thinking once. Hester's ears. How quietly, stealthily she had crept about spying on them all.

"...that McGraw fellow and Miss Collingwood sneaking around..."

"You killed them?"

She shrugged. "Not really. I just showed myself. And they died very obligingly all by themselves."

Obligingly. All by themselves. Miss Collingwood crumpled on the floor of the closet, her face a mask of horror. And John McGraw stepping back, back in terror from the walking apparition, back until he went through the glass, hurtling down to the stone terrace and death.

"...nasty liar, Miss Collingwood, saying I killed Hubert, when she knew perfectly well he died of a heart attack. Ungrateful. She didn't tell you, I suppose, how we met. I caught her shoplifting in a San Francisco department store and saved her from going to jail by bringing her here. Never mentioned it, did she?"

"No," said Jennifer. Poor, miserable, frightened Miss Collingwood had been imprisoned instead at Seacliff Pines.

"And you," Hester went on relentlessly. "I might have known you'd come galloping out.

You're like your mother who tried for years to hit me up for a loan. Greedy. You and that no good grandson of Hubert's..."

Then Alex had been speaking the truth all along.

"...wanting to *sell* Seacliff Pines..."

"But if you didn't want it sold, you could have said so in your will," Jennifer protested, close to tears.

"*That* was bait. I'm going to make a new will, one that provides a fund after I die to keep Hubert and me in this house—forever."

"I won't dispute you..."

"That's what you say now. But no matter what kind of legal paper I leave, I know darn well you— or someone else—could hire a crafty shyster to turn it around for your own selfish purpose. Leila, the bitch, got away; but she'll be taken care of, you can bet on that. My motto is, 'a dead claimant is a good claimant....'" She cackled.

The woman was not only cruel, she was mad, completely insane.

"I swear you're like that mangy cat outside," Hester complained. "Nine lives. Missed every time I tried..."

So it hadn't been John McGraw or Alex who had attempted to frighten, to harm her.

"...but this once, I'm making sure." She turned abruptly, shoving the chair aside, unlocked the door and disappeared down the corridor.

For a moment Jennifer stood paralyzed, then suddenly galvanized into life, she grabbed her raincoat and limped out into the hall and started downstairs.

"Wait!" she heard Hester shout. But Jennifer

continued her flight, not looking behind. "Wait!" Hester cried again. "If you don't, I'll blow your damn head off!"

Jennifer began to struggle with the lock on the door. A shot rang out; Jennifer heard the cracked whistle, the tinkle of glass, and she froze. For a long moment she stood pressed to the door, thinking the bullet had passed right through her, and somehow she had missed feeling it.

"Turn around!" Hester commanded.

Slowly, Jennifer obeyed. Hester stood at the head of the stairs, a revolver in her hand. "Now come back up. One funny move out of you, and I'll kill you right here."

Dry mouthed, Jennifer ascended the stairs. "Up we go," Hester said, jamming the gun into the small of her back. "Right up to the attic."

Jennifer moved down the dark corridor, her senses dulled by a vague unreality, as if her body, even her injured ankle belonged to someone else. The attic staircase went up and up, losing itself in a crowd of shadows. The gun nudged her back, and Jennifer began to climb. Near the top she stumbled, stubbing the toe of her injured foot. The pain shooting up through her leg sent the blood to her face, suddenly clearing her benumbed mind.

"This is very foolish of you, Aunt Hester," she said, marvelling at the calmness of her voice. "Alex has gone for the sheriff."

Alex. If she lived through this, she did not see how she could ever make it up to him, all the unkind words she had spoken, her scorn, her casting him in the role of imposter, thief and murderer.

"Has he now?" Hester mocked.

Time, Jennifer thought, a little time is all I need.

"Alex has not gone anywhere," Hester snickered. "Don't underestimate me. Living without a man all these years, I've learned a thing or two about cars. You don't think I'd let either of you get away? I've tinkered with the motors out there, and the first hairpin turn Alex makes—why, over he'll go." She laughed.

Jennifer, forgetting the gun turned on her. "You...you can't! All of us dying and that...that dummy which is supposed to be you. They'll find you out."

They were in the darkness of the attic now. Jennifer heard the steady, pattering rain on the roof, and she felt the wet wind as it blew in small gusts through the broken window. Hester flicked on a light, a dim bulb which hung like a glowing, conical pear from the ceiling. She waved the gun at Jennifer, and Jennifer, staring at the blue glinting steel, tried not to shudder.

"They won't find me out," Hester said. "I've told you how I've been planning this for a long time. I've made up a fool-proof story. I'll tell them Miss Collingwood thought she had killed me, but Mr. Peters replaced my supposed corpse with a dummy, then I hid in the house."

"But they..."

"Miss Collingwood won't be here to tell them differently, will she? As for McGraw and you and Alex, why all of you, in your greediness to get my estate, murdered each other."

"But," Jennifer protested, "can't you see how full of holes that story is? There's Leila Dee, for one..."

"Who's going to believe her? An aging tart who claims she saw a ghost."

"The police will want to know why you didn't come to them from the first..."

"I was too scared. Doesn't that make sense? I'm a recluse, you forget. And I was too scared to leave my hiding place."

"There's Mr. Peters," Jennifer pointed out, glad that she hadn't told Hester the old man had suffered a stroke. "He might contradict you."

But Hester was one step ahead of her. "I know Whit had a stroke. You forget, I have ears all over this house. He had a stroke, and he can't talk. Besides, he won't. The last time he pedaled up here on his bike and tried to coax me into changing my mind, I told him if he ever opened his mouth about what went on here, I'd blab too. His ex-wife is looking for him. He owes her ten thousand dollars."

Jennifer thought of the empty house and the bird cage. It seemed clear, even so, it was still an implausible, unconvincing story. And, Jennifer thought miserably, what difference does it make who disbelieves it, once I'm dead?

"I haven't got all night," Hester was saying. "I've fiddle-faddled enough. Open the window."

"No," said Jennifer, stubbornly setting her chin.

"Open the window!" Hester ordered, thrusting the gun under Jennifer's nose.

Jennifer swallowed and turned. She bent and pulled at the window. It shot up suddenly, and the rain drenched night swooped in on her. She could not see the stone terrace below, but she knew it was there. She wondered if John had died instantly or if he had lingered, his body broken, suffering agonizing pain.

Lightning flickered on the trees, flickered and held steady. Curious, strange lightning, revolving yellow, then red.

No, *not* lightning! "The sheriff!" Jennifer exclaimed joyfully, reaching up to the window frame.

"No!" Hester cried. The gun dropped, and Jennifer felt two strong hands at her back.

She hung desperately to the frame, bracing her body against Hester's push. Her fingers clawing into wood, her back arched, using all her strength as a counter force, she held fast. She felt Hester's hands weaken, and grasping the momentary lapse, she kicked back with her legs.

Hester let out a howl, and Jennifer turned in an attempt to run, brushing past her great-aunt. But the older woman caught at Jennifer's sweater with an amazing, almost super-human grip, and dragged her back to the window. Jennifer struggled, fought to free herself from Hester's iron hold that was now drawing her closer and closer to the sill. She struck out at Hester in mad, desperate fury, and for a nightmare second Jennifer saw the painted eyes of her great-aunt widen in astonishment. And then she was gone, through the window. Her scream of horror came to Jennifer thinly through the rain.

"I knew something funny was going on from the day I first got here," Alex said. The sheriff had summoned an ambulance, and it had come and gone with its grisly burdens. John McGraw was later to be identified as the wanted Jed Murphy, but for now Jennifer and Alex were sitting before a fire Alex had built against the damp cold in the front parlor. "Miss Collingwood wouldn't—or couldn't—tell me how Hester had died; Mr. Peters had made himself scarce, and you weren't talking to me. And there was that dummy upstairs made up to look like..."

"You knew all along it was a dummy?" Jennifer interrupted.

He looked at her in surprise. "Why, I thought you knew too."

"No...no. Miss Collingwood said it was a stuffed corpse, and I believed her. But I did suspect Hester was murdered."

"So did I. And I was sure her body had been hidden somewhere in the house or on the grounds. I tried finding it, but it was like looking for a needle in a haystack. And then I kept hearing footsteps. But I never could catch anyone. For a time, as I said before, I thought it was Miss Collingwood, then you, then later John McGraw, all looking for the pot of gold that was supposed to be hidden here."

"She had her money in a bank," Jennifer said. "What stumps me is how she managed to exist all these months without anyone discovering her."

"She had food, you know. All those canned goods in the attic. And she must have spent a good part of her time on the third floor. The rooms up there, for some reason, all have several doors leading one room into another, a kind of crazy quilt arrangement and an ideal hiding place."

"Her twisted scheme, all for nothing." Jennifer

sighed heavily. "Still, I wish it hadn't been me who killed her."

"It was either you or her, you know that."

"Yes," Jennifer agreed, wondering if she would ever forget that awful scream.

The fire sputtered, and sparks flew up the chimney. "I never did ask you how you made it to the sheriff," Jennifer said. "You see..."

"Because of a rock slide, I had to abandon my car at the head of the drive."

"Lucky for you. Hester had done something to the motor. You were supposed to go over the cliff at the first turn."

"She was a real charmer," he said soberly.

"Did you walk?"

"Only a half-mile. I managed to flag down a motorist who took me to a phone where I called the sheriff. He and his deputy picked me up. When we got to the drive, all three of us got out and lifted rocks and shoveled mud. The sheriff's deputy, fellow by the name of Bud Sears, kept saying, 'Can't we wait until tomorrow?' and I kept saying, 'No.' I had a feeling you might be in trouble. I'm only sorry I didn't get here sooner."

It was the first time Jennifer had heard the word "sorry" pass through Alex's lips. She looked at him, a side-long glance. His hair was still wet, darker than usual and slicked down across his skull. His nose, she noticed, had a bump in it. And there was that ugly bruise on his forehead. He did not look particularly handsome at the moment, but, she had to admit, there was still something very appealing about him.

"Now that you know I'm not a fake..." Alex grinned, "couldn't we go "halvies" on the house?"

"I don't want the house," Jennifer shivered, "not any part of it."

"Does that go for me too?" He wasn't smiling. He meant it.

"I...I don't know." His arm was thrown carelessly across the back of the sofa on which they sat. He was very close, but strangely, inexplicably, she had no desire to run from him. "Can...can I think it over?" she smiled.

"Sure," he said, leaning over and kissing her cheek tentatively, "but don't take too long."

☐ WELCOME, MY DEAR, TO BELFRY HOUSE

by Stanton Forbes

The hovering bats were only the beginning to a nightmare of terror. What horrible secrets were they hiding . . . ?

(#95322 — 95c)

☐ HOUSE OF TRAGEDY by Arlene J. Fitzgerald

A ghost mansion in an evil dream is what it looked like to Vonnie. But lately there was something nightmarish about everything in her life . . . .

(#95223 — 95c)

Manor Books Inc.
432 Park Avenue South
New York, New York 10016

Please send me the MB books I have checked above. I am enclosing $_____ Check or money order, (no currency or C.O.D.'s). Enclose price listed for each title plus 25¢ per copy ordered to cover cost of postage and handling.

☐ Send me a free list of all your books in print.

Name _____

Address _____

City_____ State_____ Zip _____

BEHIND LOCKED SHUTTERS
by
Dan Ross

The romantic chalet was beautiful and dream-like and Elizabeth felt like royalty. But when the cries of ghostly madness echoed through the shadowy halls, the dream became a nightmare. . . .

95376—95¢

PAMELA'S PALACE
by
Arlene J. Fitzgerald

Pamela meant to turn her family's old mansion into a home once again. But she could not fathom its dark secrets or overcome the horrid creature determined to destroy her. . . .

95377—95¢

THE BIGAMOUS DUCHESS
by Muriel Elwood

A magnificent novel of the Royal Court. The whole of London was at the feet of the fiery and beautiful Elizabeth until a scandal threatened her downfall.

15144—$1.50

DEATH IS MY SHADOW
by Edward S. Aarons

All Pete wanted was a woman. He found plenty—every one beautiful to behold and dangerous to the touch. Soon, Pete's innocent fancies became a trapdoor to brutality and ever-widening circles of death.

95371—95¢
